The c

The bi-plane  below them. As they flew over Main Street, the plane rose to a higher altitude.

She peered from side to side observing the earth from a perspective she'd never dreamed about. The thick green forests would open to a lake or pasture then another forest would come into view. The vibration of the bi-plane swept through her body, dulling her senses. She closed her eyes and relaxed against the seat. She had no idea how long they'd been in the air.

The humming of the wires changed to a higher pitch. The airplane picked up speed. She grabbed the sides of the seat as fear clutched her heart. She closed her eyes and prayed. The bi-plane hit the pasture with a bounce before coming to a stop close to the shed.

Victor turned off the engine. He stepped out, climbed on the plane beside the seat and reached for Dottie's hand to help her out.

He jumped off the wing, grabbed her around the waist, and set her in front of him. Without saying a word, he took her face in his hands. He bent to kiss her. Her legs were weak from flying. She hadn't gotten used to being on land. When he kissed her, it was as if she were in a whirlpool, the earth spinning around her.

She swayed, Victor steadied her. "Well, how do you like it?"

She tightened her hold on his arm as the earth turned beneath her. "What, the flying?"

He pulled the aviator cap off her head. "Yes, the flying."

"I was scared at first, but when we got in the air, I relaxed and enjoyed the ride."

Kudos for Jane Lewis

LOVE AT FIVE THOUSAND FEET was a finalist in the Hearts Through History chapter of Romance Writers of America in their 2016 Romance Through The Ages Contest, Post Victorian/World War II category.

Love & Air!
In the Air
Jane Lewis

Love at Five Thousand Feet

by

Jane Lewis

This is a work of fiction. Names, characters, places, and incidents are either the product of the author's imagination or are used fictitiously, and any resemblance to actual persons living or dead, business establishments, events, or locales, is entirely coincidental.

Love at Five Thousand Feet

COPYRIGHT © 2017 by Pamela Hudson

All rights reserved. No part of this book may be used or reproduced in any manner whatsoever without written permission of the author or The Wild Rose Press, Inc. except in the case of brief quotations embodied in critical articles or reviews.
Contact Information: info@thewildrosepress.com

Cover Art by *Debbie Taylor*

The Wild Rose Press, Inc.
PO Box 708
Adams Basin, NY 14410-0708
Visit us at www.thewildrosepress.com

Publishing History
First Vintage Rose Edition, 2017
Print ISBN 978-1-5092-1714-4
Digital ISBN 978-1-5092-1715-1

Published in the United States of America

Dedication

This book is dedicated to my brother Jim,
whose knowledge, expertise,
and love of flying airplanes
from the Stearman biplane of yesterday
to the Lockheed C-5 Galaxy of today
was the inspiration for this book.
You paved every road I have taken,
and for that I am grateful.

Chapter One

Saplingville, Georgia, 1934

The JN-4 Jenny bi-plane dove straight for Uncle Walter's pig pen. Victor Douglas turned in his seat and yelled, "Pull back Frankie, what're ya trying to do, kill us?" He tightened his seat belt and grabbed the sides of his seat. The bi-plane rose and leveled off at five thousand feet. He relaxed in his seat until the barnstormer turned the plane over in a barrel roll. "Damn it, Frankie." His screams and yells were drowned out by the roar of the engine and the humming of the wires.

He closed his eyes and took a deep breath as the crazy man stopped the barrel rolls and kept the bi-plane at a nice cruising altitude. The plane went straight into a figure eight. He didn't like his bi-plane in the hands of a daredevil. His breathing returned to normal as the plane headed for the landing strip next to the corn field.

He stared at the ground. Uncle Walter waved his straw hat. The old man was their airport tower. When they took off, he removed the chocks and propped the plane and when they landed, he helped with the tie down.

He watched the landing strip loom closer as the plane touched down in the perfect three point landing the aviator was famous for. He breathed a sigh of relief as they rolled to their tie down spot.

Victor climbed out of the front seat and jumped to the ground. "Frankie, you're not a barnstormer anymore. Those days are over. I swear if you crash my plane or kill us, I'll kill you!"

The former stunt pilot jumped off the wing and removed his hat and goggles. "The Jenny was mine first."

"Yeah and I paid you." He softened his voice, "I can't help it if you went through the money as fast as crap through a goose. You're lucky I let you fly my plane."

"So I'll get to fly the Jenny again, huh?" Frankie rubbed his hand along the tail of the plane.

A stab of guilt pierced through his gut, the Jenny was the only thing his best friend cared about. "Maybe, if you'll stop showing off. If not, find your own flying circus."

Walter joined in the conversation. "That's right Frankie, my hens won't lay for a week now, besides you scared Delores so bad she went to bed. I know you boys like to have fun, but there is a limit here."

Frankie shook Walter's hand. "Sorry Mr. Andrews, I got carried away, she flies so smooth I couldn't help myself. I miss my barnstorming days."

A sarcastic smirk crossed his friend's face. "You miss showing off. We're not kids anymore, and chances are not what I want to take with my life, or my plane." Victor crossed his arms daring him to start a fight.

"You think because you learned to fly in the United States Army Air Corp, you're a better pilot than me. Hell, you even think you are a better man than I am." Frankie pushed Victor's chest with his hands.

He didn't back off. He moved closer. "I don't want to die, and I can't afford to buy another plane."

Walter walked between them. "Boys, let's calm down, no sense in saying things you don't mean."

He gazed down, he couldn't look his uncle in the eye. "Sorry, Uncle Walter, thanks for your help."

Frankie shuffled his feet. "Yeah, Mr. Andrews, sorry and thanks."

The older man glared at the two men. "There's no sense in your arguing. You've been best friends since you were little boys. You're both good pilots, in your own way. I'd fly with either one of you. Now go on with yourselves, I'm going to check on my wife."

Victor double checked the tie downs. They walked through the field in the direction of the house and driveway.

He slowed his walk; they shouldn't go home mad. "Hey, I remember the day you joined the barnstormer team."

Frankie smiled. "Yeah, they didn't want anything to do with a fifteen year old country bumpkin like me. I almost got down on my knees and begged them before they said they'd let me go with 'em. They worked my ass off. Guess they figured I'd either step up or leave."

He studied his friend. "Guess you showed them, huh? When they disbanded you were the star of the show."

Frankie held his chin high. "Well, I learned from the ground up. I can't tell you how many times I pulled chocks for taxi or how many propellers I propped. When they found out I knew more about the engine than the mechanic, they taught me to fly. The greatest day of my life. The saddest day was when they disbanded and I flew my Jenny back here."

"It certainly gets in your blood. I hated to leave the service, I enjoyed flying the military planes." Victor reached for the cat asleep on his car and placed it on the ground.

They climbed in the car. Victor rolled his window down and pulled the door up with his right hand while holding the handle with his left. He heard the click of the door catching in the latch and started the car. He backed his 1925 Buick out of the gravel driveway. "Today was a nice day to fly. Did you see the people at the park watch as we flew over?"

Frankie smiled and peered into the sky. "I know what they're thinking. How in the world did the airplane get off the ground?"

"That's what they always ask me."

Frankie turned toward Victor. "Hey, we could sell rides in the plane. We could make lots of money flying people around town."

He didn't want to disappoint his friend, but he had to tell him where he stood on the matter. "We could, but I'm not interested and it's my airplane. My idea of flying people around is in a commercial airliner, not my bi-plane."

Frankie lowered his voice. "So, when are you leavin'?"

He stopped at a stop sign and turned left onto the paved country road. "I've been making some inquiries. I'm working on it."

"What are you waitin' for? I keep hearing about your plans, but I see no action."

"You want me to go?"

"Well if you do, can I buy my plane back?"

He eased off on the clutch after putting the car in the last gear. "Did they raise your salary at Spangler Cotton Mill, or you gonna rob a bank, because last I heard you were broke."

"I'll get there one day. I won't always be a mill hand." Frankie stared out the car window into the distance.

Victor conceded, "You're right though. I need to start making plans."

"With your experience, you won't have trouble getting a job flying. I should have gone in the Army Air Corp with you. Back then, I was too busy flying Jenny's around the country. I had fun, but look at me now. All I know how to do is fly a bi-plane. Barnstormers aren't in demand anymore."

His best friend needed confidence. "For what it's worth, I've flown with the best pilots in the Army Air Corp and no one comes close to your skills. It's not too late for you to learn how to fly the new ships."

Frankie closed his eyes and took a deep breath. "I hope you're right."

He remembered their life together. It hadn't been long since they were in grammar school taking up for each other if a fight broke out. *Why did Frankie take chances with his life? He didn't have to prove anything to him, they were more brothers than friends.*

The car dipped as he turned off the paved road onto the dirt road in the direction of the shanty town. Victor slowed the car and avoided holes as rocks and dirt flew from the wheels. He put on brakes and eased the clutch in as they cranked the windows so the dirt wouldn't sail into the car. The houses came into view. He navigated the road so he wouldn't side swipe the cars parked in the small front yards. Even with the windows closed they could smell the outhouses. He slammed on his brakes as a little boy chased a chicken across the road. Most people sat on their front porches to stay cool. They waved as they drove by. He thanked God he had a good family and a nice house to live in. He regretted their argument, he wanted Frankie to be successful and escape his life of poverty.

"Thanks, Victor. I did enjoy the day, and I know you enjoyed my barnstorming tricks."

He waved his friend out of the car. "Get out of here, you crazy man. See you next week."

The sun headed for the horizon when he arrived in town. The few street lights in Saplingville glowed waiting for the dark. His favorite time of day, he drove slowly watching the sky change colors.

Even though the last few minutes of their flight had been harrowing, they had a perfect day for flying. The two hours spent in the sky seemed like two minutes. He never tired of being in the air. In the open cockpit of the Jenny soaring above the earth, he enjoyed a freedom and peace. The sensation stayed with him long after he landed.

He drove slowly through town savoring the memories of his day in the air when a flash of yellow took him from his thoughts. A young woman in a yellow dress walked toward him. He slowed and turned his head. The car drifted too close to the sidewalk and he swerved to the left. He got the old jalopy under control and stopped at the side of the road. His headlights framed the girl as she walked toward him. Her long wavy hair and curvy figure drew his attention. She climbed the steps to the Boarding House and sat on the swing with Ella Simons. He reached for the door handle, then stopped. He didn't need any complications, and a pretty girl like her could derail his plan of leaving town.

He would be an airline pilot come hell or high water.

His responsibility to his family had kept him in town too long already.

Chapter Two

Dottie made her way to the two story white clapboard house known as Ella's Boarding House. The land lady lived in the attic room and rented out the other six bedrooms in the house. Dottie and her father rented two of the rooms. The woman scooted over in the swing making room for her.

Ella Simons pursed her lips. "Avery's not here. Never came home today."

She grabbed Ella's hand. "He hasn't been here all day?"

"He left early this morning and I haven't seen him since. Take a deep breath and calm down. I'm sure he'll be along."

She closed her eyes and prayed her daddy would come home. The swing swayed as they pushed with their feet. The soft glow of lightning bugs blinked in the night. The night breeze drifted through the porch and up Dottie's skirt as the swing moved back and forth. The coolness of the air almost made her forget about the sweltering heat of the day.

She stared into the night. "I wish Daddy would stop drinking and get a job. I thought after Mama died moving to his home town would be better. Now I'm not so sure."

Ella turned. "Maybe he hoped he could keep Carolyn's memory alive here. I'm sure he misses her."

"Daddy can't miss Mama more than I do. She loved him way more than he loved her, and he knew she did. He hasn't been able to hold a job and his drinking's worse since we moved here."

Ella patted her hand. "Give him time, he'll come around. Your daddy has a lot of guilt to work through."

Dottie stopped the swing. "He should feel guilty about the way he treated her. She knew he had other women."

The swing moved sideways until Ella put her foot on the porch to steady it. She pushed with her feet until the swing straightened, rocking with a gentle flow. She reflected on her life with Avery and his wife. "Carolyn was my friend, we all went to school together. She was a sweet girl, and smart too. All of us girls were in love with Avery, but when he set his sights on her, there was no use for us to even try."

"Did he love her?"

Ella nodded. "Oh, yes, he loved Carolyn."

"What was Daddy like before he started his drinking?"

"Handsome, even as a little boy. None of us had money. We were all poor farmer or mill worker kids, but somehow, he found clothes a little different, or fancier than anyone else. A charmer, could talk the horns off a billy goat, and make you believe anything."

Dottie put her feet on the porch and stopped the swing. "My aunt wants me to move to Macon with her, but she told me Daddy isn't welcome." A tear streamed down her face. The lump in her throat made her words come out in a whisper. "He keeps telling me he'll stop drinking and get a job. How can I leave him after I promised Mama I'd take care of him?"

Ella took her hand. "I believe you have to do what makes you happy, and if it's leaving him to fend for himself, that's what you have to do."

A shadow caught her eye. She stared as the form of a man materialized on the sidewalk. Her heart sank with recognition when he stumbled over his own feet. "I see him." She jumped. The swing went sideways leaving Ella to steady it. She ran down the sidewalk and took her daddy's arm.

Avery swayed and mumbled something hard to understand. "I couldn't find Carolyn, I don't know where she is." A hot poker went through her heart. Drunk again. He doesn't even remember Mama died.

She led her father up the front walk to the boarding house.

Avery straightened and turned his head. He squinted, a glimmer of recognition filled his eyes. "Hey baby girl, how ya doin'? Oh, I feel sick."

Ella ran down the steps. "Avery, not on my zinnias. Oh, Good Lord, Dottie you bring him in. I'll get a wet rag."

She pulled her daddy close and wrapped her arms around his ribcage to steady him. "Lean on me, I'll help you in."

"You're the best baby girl, what'd I do without you? Sweet as your mama was, that's what you are."

She guided him in the front door, to his room on the right. He kicked over the umbrella bucket. Ella set it right and put the umbrellas into it.

His lanky body proved too heavy for her to handle. "Ella can you help me get him in the bed?"

Ella ran in the bedroom and pulled the string on the overhead light. She grabbed Avery's arm, put it over her shoulder and helped guide him into the bedroom. "Sit him on the bed and I'll take his shoes off." The older lady untied his shoes and yanked.

He fell on the bed. They raised his feet and straightened him out the best they could.

Dottie brushed the hair from his face. Tears dripped from her eyes. *What if I lose him, too?* She pulled her skirt and wiped the salty water from her face with the stiff material. "Oh, Daddy, why do you do this?"

Ella went in the bathroom, grabbed a rag, and wet it. She stood in the door watching. "Here you go. Call me if you need anything."

She took the rag and washed her daddy's face. "I will, thanks for your help."

She pulled the string on the overhead light and sat in the straight chair beside the bed. Enough light from the moon came through the window for her to see Avery's chest rising with each breath. When her daddy went to sleep after drinking, she always checked to see if he was breathing because he stayed passed out too long.

Dottie said softly. "Daddy, I'm twenty years old. My girlfriends are married with babies. I have a job and support you, but what do you do? You get drunk. You won't work. I love you but you aren't going to treat me like you did Mama."

Avery started snoring. She stared into the darkness and remembered her mother. She was sixteen when her mama got sick. The three years she took care of her seemed ages ago. Carolyn loved Avery. She made Dottie promise to take care of him when she died. Her eyes moved to the ceiling of the room. "That wasn't fair, Mama. He's worse now you aren't here."

She fell asleep in the chair next to her daddy's bed. She woke when her head fell against the chair. She forced her eyes open and stretched her arms before standing. She backed out of the room staring at her father and closed the door without a sound. She made her way upstairs to get her things ready for work the next day.

Dottie woke to the sound of the Spangler Cotton Mill bell. It reminded her of what her life could be like. She thanked God she got a job at Murphy's Five and Dime and not the Cotton Mill. She fastened her brassiere and grabbed her knickers noticing the frayed seam that needed mending. No time for sewing this morning, she stepped into her most comfortable dress. She pulled the thick cotton stockings up to her thigh and fastened the garter wishing she could afford the cooler nylons. Leaving her room in disarray, she ran downstairs to check on her father.

"Daddy, are you awake?" She pushed the door open.

"Yeah, you can come in."

He sat on the side of the bed holding his head in his hands. "Oh, baby girl, I don't feel good today."

He stood and lost his balance. Dottie grabbed him and pushed him toward the bed. "Get in bed, I'll get you some coffee."

He grabbed her hand, "No, sit and talk to me, don't leave."

"I have to go to work, and I'm gonna be late."

Avery struggled, "My baby girl doesn't have to work, I'll take care of you."

She took a pillow off the chair. "Here lean on this

pillow. I'll get you some coffee."

Dottie walked into the kitchen. She and Ella watched two squirrels chase each other around a pine tree. Ella's face appeared paler than usual. She smelled the faint smell of bourbon. "Will you give Daddy some coffee and don't let him leave the house today. I have to go, or I'm going to be late for work."

Ella assured her. "I'll take care of everything, don't worry."

She left the house as Ella poured a cup for Avery, and headed to his room.

She knocked on the door. "Avery, it's me Ella, I've brought coffee for you."

"You can come in. Where's Dottie?"

She entered the room and sat the coffee cup and a plate with toast on the bedside table. "She went to work."

Avery sat and managed to swing his legs to the floor. "She doesn't have to work, I can take care of her. Tell her to come back. Help me." Avery struggled, the mattress clinging like quick sand.

"Stay in the bed Avery, you're not well." She hurried to his bedside.

With her help he returned to his place propped against the pillows. "Sweet Ella, you've always been a good girl."

"Drink the coffee. The toast will make your stomach better. I brought you an aspirin. Take it."

Ella walked over to the window and raised the shade. "Dottie wants you to stay here until she gets home tonight."

Avery reached for the coffee cup. "My baby girl had to grow up too fast."

She turned from the window. "You can say that again. I don't want to put my nose where it doesn't belong, but right now, all I see is her taking care of you."

He tilted his head and glared. "What do you mean?"

Ella waked to the door and turned. "I mean you've been on a bender since you came back to town. If you want to help her, you've got to stop drinking."

Avery sipped his coffee trying to keep his hands steady. "I'm gonna do better."

Chapter Three

Victor knocked on his parents' bedroom door, "Pa, you feel like walking to work this morning?"

Jacob's footsteps clipped hard on the floor. "Yes, I'll be ready in five minutes."

He walked down the stairs, and out the front screen door. He stood on the porch, the humidity making his shirt stick to his skin. Clear skies and no wind, a perfect day to fly. He didn't look forward to another minute in the hot drug store with his father.

Jacob came out, letting the screen door slam. "Let's go."

When they reached the end of their road and headed to Main Street, the sidewalks became wider. Most of the houses were shaded by large oak trees in the front. The only sounds were a few cars passing by and car horns. They waved as people stuck their heads out of the automobiles and said hello. Jacob had been the town pharmacist for years and everyone knew him. Victor shuttered as he remembered Frankie and most of the towns people working in the stuffy loud Cotton Mill. They reached Main Street and walked down the alley to the back door of the drug store. Jacob turned the key in the lock, pushing on the door to open it. Inside, he turned on the lights before heading for the pharmacy counter. Victor walked to the front, unlocked the door and turned the closed sign to open. The same routine for the last year and a half.

He wanted to move on. He was a trained pilot, not a soda jerk. Helping out as a teenager was different, it gave him extra money for dates and flying lessons but a soda jerk and gofer for his father at twenty-four years old was unacceptable. In his spare time, he stared out the window day dreaming about flying. He organized food for the lunch crowd and watched Jacob sort and bottle medicine. *I told him I was leaving and to find someone to help but I haven't seen any indication he is. I should be flying an airplane, not cutting lemons.*

Victor noticed a girl race by the front window. *Same girl from last night.* He rushed to the window as she entered Murphy's Five and Dime. He waited for her to come out, but she didn't. He sauntered to the soda fountain glancing toward the Five and Dime every chance he got. Later in the afternoon, he decided to take a break, and mosey over to Murphy's.

Victor walked into the Five and Dime, and let his eyes adjust to the light. He spotted the owner sitting at his desk. "Hi, Mr. Murphy, how are you today?"

"Fine, Victor. How's Mr. Douglas?"

"He's doing well, thank you."

He searched the store. The pretty girl stood two aisles over unpacking a box of nail files. He watched her work. She glanced at him, their eyes locked. He smiled and watched as her cheeks flushed red. "Good afternoon."

"Hi, may I help you with something today?" She dropped the empty box on the floor along with several nail files. She stooped over, gathered the nail files, and returned them to the display while kicking the box behind the counter with her foot.

Victor gave her a good look over. "I'd like to buy some candy." He walked with her to the candy counter.

She smiled but she didn't look him in the eye. "Of course, what would you like?"

Her hand shook as she opened the sliding glass door. "How about a quarter pound of peppermint?" She put a few sticks on the scale, aiming for exactly a quarter pound. She gave a sigh of relief when he said. "That amount's fine."

She raised her head and smiled. He smiled back. "How long have you worked here? I don't believe I've seen you before."

She put the candy in a bag. "We got into town two weeks ago, I've worked here a week. My father's from here. Avery Lester? I'm Dottie."

He extended his hand and she placed hers in his. He shook her hand but he had an urge to kiss it instead. "Well Miss Lester, it's nice to meet you. I'm Victor Douglas. I work at Douglas Drug Store. My father is Jacob, the pharmacist and owner. Where do you live?" He gave her a quarter.

She moved to the cash register for his change. "We're at Ella's Boarding House right now. As soon as Daddy gets a job, we're moving to a house of our own."

Mr. Murphy called from the back of the store, "Dottie there's a box of men's handkerchiefs that needs emptying."

She walked toward Mr. Murphy's desk then turned. "It was nice to meet you. I have to get to work."

Victor put a piece of peppermint in his mouth and stayed rooted to the spot as she hurried to get the box. A surprised expression washed over her face when she walked to the front of the store. "Bye, Dottie Lester, I'll

see you around."
   She rested her gaze on him. "Bye, Victor Douglas."

Chapter Four

Victor polished the counter while Jacob locked the money in a safe. He swept the linoleum floor, then opened the front door and brushed the sidewalk gazing across the street. He hoped to get another glimpse of Dottie. Instead, a couple of giggling teenagers went in the Five and Dime. He locked the front door, hung the closed sign, and grabbed a mop and bucket. His father sat at his desk reviewing the drug inventory. Careful not to leave footprints on the clean floor, he wrung out the mop and poured the mop water in the toilet. "Ready to go, Pa?"

Jacob pushed some papers into a drawer. "Yes, we're done for the day."

The thick wooden door was hard to close but Victor knew the trick. He secured the door. Jacob inserted the key and turned it. They walked to the front of the store and crossed Main Street.

They walked past Murphy's Five and Dime. He hesitated staring through the thick glass. He heard his father talking but he didn't pay attention. "I'm sorry, did you say something?"

Jacob glared at his son. "I said the drug store will be yours someday. You should go to school to be a pharmacist. You'll make more money if you run the store, and dispense medicine too. I want a stable career for you. The drug store's been good for Henrietta and me."

Victor's pulse beat faster, the blood flowing to his face. He didn't want to disappoint his father, but he had to set the record straight. "Pa, I thought you were searching for my replacement. I told you when I came back I didn't want to stay here."

Jacob stopped, and contemplated his son. "I don't understand why you came back in the first place. I knew when you left you'd come home thinking we weren't good enough for you."

He unclenched his fists and put his hand on his father's arm, "It's not that. I have plans."

Jacob pulled away. "Flying around the country is dangerous. How about when you have a family? Do you want to put your wife through worrying about you every day you go to work?"

"Pa, I'm a trained pilot. I flew bomber planes in the United States Army Air Corp."

Jacob stopped in his tracks. "All I've seen you do since you returned is fly through town in your run down airplane with Frankie, doing tricks and trying to get yourself killed."

He stared at his father. "Well, I'm sorry, but I'm not backing down, so you better find someone to help you, and soon." *I should have never returned to Saplingville. He would have already hired someone to help by now. By staying the last year, he believes I don't want to leave. Pa's right, flying a commercial airline is very different from a Jenny, if I don't act soon I won't have any skills to offer.*

Victor wouldn't say anything else. He didn't want to argue. He noticed his father breathing hard and slowed his pace. "Are you okay?"

Jacob nodded. "I can't walk as fast as I used to."

His father struggled to catch his breath. Victor continued to watch him and let his pa determine the walking pace.

As they ambled up the front walk to the house, he smelled Ma's meat loaf. The rich smell of onions and spices along with the sound of his youngest sister, Lisbeth, practicing the piano overwhelmed him. He should enjoy these precious moments with his family, he'd miss them. Victor walked in the house and noticed his middle sister, Ruth Ann, sprawled out on the sofa reading her Theatre Arts Monthly Magazine.

"Ruth Ann Douglas, come in the kitchen now, and help me get supper on the table." Ma said, more like a command than a request.

He stood at the door and watched Ruth Ann ignore their mother.

She sat, stuck her tongue out and waved her magazine in the air. "What? I can't even read?"

"Go help Ma, please."

She stood and slowly walked toward to the kitchen. "I'm going. Someday soon I'll be out of here and I'll do exactly what I want."

Victor swatted her on the backside. "You pretty much do that now." He followed Ruth Ann into the kitchen, took plates out of the cabinet and passed them to her before he opened the utensil drawer. He tickled her but she ran to the other side of the room. He put the forks and knives next to the plates and chased her around the table until his father entered the doorway with his arms crossed.

Jacob gave them a stern look. "What's this ruckus going on? This is a place to eat, not play."

They stood at their chairs waiting for their parents to sit. Jacob sat at the head of the table and Hattie at the other end. Lisbeth entered the room and took her seat.

Jacob nodded toward his wife. "Henrietta, please say thanks."

As soon as Hattie blessed the food, she took a piece of meatloaf off the platter and passed it to Victor.

He took an extra piece. "Ma, this is my favorite, thanks for making it."

She passed the bowls of green beans, mashed potatoes, sliced tomatoes, and cornbread. "When you were in the service and we had meatloaf for supper, it made us miss you more."

"I missed y'all too, especially your cookin'. California's a long way from Georgia and the food there isn't the same."

"Heavens, it's a wonder you didn't starve to death."

He put a big spoonful of green beans on his plate. "Did the vegetables come from Uncle Walter?"

"Yes, Delores brought the green beans and tomatoes to the Women's Missionary Union meeting. She picked them yesterday."

Jacob chose a piece of cornbread and put butter on it. "How'd the meeting go?"

"A disaster. I figured it would be easier since I'm president this year, but you know Clara…always has to stick her nose in."

"For a preacher's wife, she sure is a busybody." Jacob took a bite of cornbread.

"She sure is. I want us to make a quilt to auction off for the children's home. She wants to have a bake sale."

"Why not do both?"

"That's what one of the ladies said. Clara shook her head and said no, we're only going to do the bake sale. Well, Emma Harris got up and left the meeting. Emma's been saving flour sacks the past year for the quilt."

"Henrietta, you're the president, all you have to do is ask the group to vote. Clara doesn't have the last word." Jacob reached for his tea glass.

Hattie jumped from her chair, and grabbed a pencil and paper. "You're right, Jacob. I'll put it on my agenda for next week."

Victor wiped his mouth with his napkin. "Good supper, Ma."

Hattie finished writing herself a note and sat in her chair. "Thanks, did you have a good day?"

"I did. Hey, do you remember an Avery Lester? His daughter works at Murphy's. I met her today. Her name is Dottie."

She put her fork down. "Avery Lester married Carolyn Rowe right after high school. I heard they had a daughter, but haven't seen them since they moved away." She lowered her voice, "I don't know a lot about them but I heard he had a drinking problem and…"

Victor took control of the conversation, he didn't like where it was going. "Dottie didn't mention her mother, but she told me she and Mr. Lester moved to town a couple of weeks ago. They live at Ella's Boarding House."

Jacob wiped his mouth with the cloth napkin. "I remember Avery's father. A good man, real honest, too bad Avery didn't take after him."

"Who wants to go to the picture show tonight?" Ruth Ann pushed her plate away.

Jacob gave her a stern look. "What movie's playing this week?"

"*The Invisible Man*," she said with an air of defiance.

Hattie put her hand on her chest. "Dear me, doesn't sound like the sort of movie you should be seeing."

Ruth Ann nodded at her brother and raised her eyebrows. "Victor will go with me, won't you? Lisbeth has a piano lesson tonight. I'm dying to see Gloria Stuart."

Lisbeth scrunched her nose, "I wouldn't go to that movie even if I didn't have a piano lesson. It sounds scary. Who ever heard of an invisible man?"

"You're not an expert on the theater or movies." Ruth Ann stood and took her plate to the sink.

"I'll go with you, but first the dishes have to be done, and kitchen cleaned." Victor took his father's plate and raked scraps into the trash can.

He and Ruth Ann worked together to finish their job. He peeked out of the kitchen into the living room. Jacob relaxed in his favorite chair. He quietly went to his room to change clothes. He didn't want another confrontation with his father about his future. Ruth Ann waited on the front porch. He carefully closed the screen door and they headed to his car. "I'm going to stop by Frankie's house, to see if he wants to go."

His sister got in the car and slammed the door. "Why do you have to ask him? He's a smart aleck. I don't like the way he looks at me."

"Be nice, he's had a rough life, things are hard right now. Besides he's my best friend and I want him to go."

"He's a mill hand. You always hang out with low class people. You better stay away from the drunk's daughter."

Victor slanted an eye her way. "She seemed nice enough."

Ruth Ann dug something out of her pocketbook. At first, he couldn't believe she had a pack of Lucky Strike cigarettes. He collected his thoughts before he spoke. "Hey, where did you get those?"

She pulled out a box of matches and said, "I'm sixteen. I can smoke if I want to."

"Let me have one." He took the pack and stuck the cigarettes in his pocket.

"Hey, give those back." She reached out to grab them.

"Nope, you're not getting them." Victor pushed Ruth Ann in her seat. "I also heard you sneak out of the house the other night. Do it again and I'll come after you. The only reason I don't tell Ma is because I don't want to upset Pa. He's not feeling well lately."

She snapped her pocketbook closed. "Yeah, and you want to skip out on all of us. You can't wait to leave again."

He pulled the cigarettes from his pocket and threw them out the window. "I'm twenty-four years old and already left town once, and it's time to get on with my life. You'll be leaving soon yourself."

"Hey, why'd you do that? Now I have to buy another pack." She threw her bag into the rear seat, "When you pick up Frankie, I'm getting in the back and ducking my head I don't want to be seen in his company."

"Like the crowd you hang out with is better. I threw them out as a warning to you. If I see you with another pack, I'm telling."

Victor eased the car down the rutted dirt road toward Frankie's house.

"You're going to ruin your car coming here. He's probably not even home."

He slowed, Frankie sat on his porch.

He walked to the car, and peered through Victor's window. "How's Ruthie doin'?"

"It's Ruth Ann to you." She folded her arms staring straight ahead.

Victor took the car out of gear, let off the clutch and held the car still with his foot on the brake. "Came to see if you want to go to the picture show with us."

"Absolutely." He walked around the car and opened the door. Ruth Ann jumped into the bench seat in the back.

Frankie settled in the front seat. "What movie's playing?"

"*The Invisible Man*. Ruth Ann wants to see Gloria Stuart."

"Me too, you won't see much of Claude Rains because he'll be invisible."

Ruth Ann leaned toward the front seat. "Frankie, I'm surprised you know the names of the movie stars."

He turned, their eyes locked. "I'm not stupid, I know more than you think I do."

Victor glared at his sister and turned to Frankie. "All right you two, be nice to each other."

He parked the car in front of the theater. As soon as he opened his door, his sister jumped out and ran to meet her friends. Clearly the leader of the pack. The other kids moved aside letting her enter their inner circle. They all started talking at once and Ruth Ann raised her hand to silence them. She walked over to one of the boys and whispered in his ear. She and the boy started walking toward the theater and the others followed except one of the girls stormed off. "Did you see what just happened? She took the girl's boyfriend." Victor walked faster so he could find a seat close enough to watch his sister and her friend during the movie.

Frankie shook his head. "I saw it. She's getting prettier every day. I wish she'd like me."

"Well right now, she only cares about Ruth Ann. I hope she lives to be twenty-one."

"What's she doing?"

"Smoking, sneaking out at night, lying to my parents, you name it. If I were you, I wouldn't mention you like her."

"It wouldn't do me any good now, would it?"

They sat in the back of the packed theater a few seats behind his sister. The theater smelled like stale popcorn and cigarette smoke. The light of the projector flashed on the screen and the sound of the film sputtering around the wheel brought a quiet hush. The lights dimmed, the projector started working on the second try.

The movie flashed on the screen. Victor watched Ruth Ann's group settle into their seats. The boy she sat with put his arm around her and pulled her close. He grinned as she took his arm from her neck and placed it in his lap. Her head remained straight ahead focusing on the screen and the special effects. When Dr. Griffin went on his killing spree you could hear gasps.

After the movie, Victor and Frankie gathered with people outside the theater. Everyone gave their opinions on how they made Dr. Griffin invisible. Ruth Ann and her friends gathered in a tight circle whispering to each other.

Victor murmured under his breath, "Probably making plans to sneak out tonight."

"Yeah, you better watch her. She'll get into real trouble." Frankie stared at the teenagers.

Ruth Ann headed to the car. She nodded to her brother. "Let's go boys."

Victor started the car and turned. "I hope you weren't making plans to meet them later. I told you, you're not sneaking out on my watch."

"Don't be silly. I don't sneak. How about the movie? Can you believe Dr. Griffin made himself invisible?"

Frankie faced Ruth Ann. "Yep, he had a good thing going, until he started killing people. I can see the advantage of being invisible."

He couldn't believe their take on the film. "Have you both lost your mind? The man messed with something he shouldn't, and ruined people's lives, then ultimately lost his own. Not unlike you, little sister, if you don't wise up."

He intentionally turned on the street leading to Ella's Boarding House hoping he would see Dottie. He slowed his car to a crawl and leaned forward. She sat on the front porch with a man and Miss Simons. *The man must be Mr. Lester.* From the glare of the porch light, he watched her talk and laugh. He yearned to be a part of their conversation.

Ruth Ann leaned over the front seat. "I told you to

leave the drunk's daughter alone."

Frankie perked up, "What drunk's daughter?"

"Oh, I met a girl today. She moved to town a couple of weeks ago and works at Murphy's."

Ruth Ann spoke, "Her daddy's making a name for himself, probably one of your friends."

"Why would he be a friend of mine?" Frankie glared at her.

She gave him a smug grin and raised an eyebrow. "Because he's a white trash drunk, like you."

Victor stopped the car. "Ruth Ann, enough. Apologize to Frankie. Now."

She rolled her eyes. "I'm sorry Frankie."

Frankie laughed, but her words hit below the belt. Mr. Howard, Frankie's father drank too much. When Frankie's mother died, Mr. Howard left town, and Frankie never saw him again. Frankie'd been on his own since he was fifteen.

Victor turned down the dirt road and parked in front of the old shanty house. "This is your stop Frankie. How about Sunday dinner with us at Uncle Walter's house? We need to work on the engine, and do some flying in the afternoon."

"Absolutely. Thanks for the ride into town." Frankie stepped out of the car and stuck his head through the open window. "Bye, Ruthie."

She stuck her tongue out.

Frankie climbed the one step to the porch and waved.

Victor nodded and went on his way.

He turned. "Ruth Ann, why do you have to be so cruel to people? Frankie has never been anything but nice to you."

"I'll tell you why. Frankie's a dumb mill hand, why do you hang out with him?"

"Frankie is not dumb. He's a very smart man, honest and hard working, more than I see from those boys you hang out with."

They arrived home and Victor cringed as his sister slammed the car door. He jumped out of the car. "Remember, I'll be listening for you. If you sneak out tonight, I'll come looking for you, you hear me?"

They walked to the front porch. He grabbed the screen door before she slammed it in his face.

Hattie came out of the living room. "Did you enjoy the movie?"

Ruth Ann smiled at Victor. "The movie was great."

How can she change from an inconsiderate girl, who almost closed the door in my face, to a smiling, innocent sweet girl in a matter of seconds? He hugged his mother. "The special effects made it worth seeing."

Ruth Ann headed to the kitchen. "Yes, I couldn't wait to see how they would make an invisible man."

Hattie followed her. "How'd they make him invisible?"

"The man wore clothes, bandages, and goggles so he appeared normal until he took them off, then you couldn't see anything of him at all."

He listened hoping his sister would leave the part out about the man's killing spree, or how he died. He smiled and went upstairs to his room. He turned on his lamp and rested on his bed with his hands behind his head gazing at the ceiling. He had to get out of Saplingville.

He wanted to fly commercial Stinson T Tri-Motors and possibly the new Douglas DC-2's. He enjoyed the camaraderie with the other pilots. Pilots understood each other. They faced danger ever day. He'd been in situations where the weather changed and he had to rely on instruments to fly the plane. He loved the excitement of flying a new ship, as they called their planes, and discovering the new gages and instruments.

Victor pulled out his *Flying Aces* magazine and read the advertisement for Delta Air Corporation. The airline flew mail service out of Atlanta. They were going to resume passenger service, and change their name to Delta Air Lines. He would take this chance to get in at the beginning of their commercial venture. He walked to the window, and gazed at the sky. No clouds, only stars and a sliver of moon. He loved the vastness of space.

He sat at his desk and took out a pen and paper. He wrote a letter to Delta Air Lines in Atlanta, requesting a job interview. He sealed the envelope and rummaged through the top drawer for a stamp. He would take the letter to the post office tomorrow.

Chapter Five

Dottie hunted through her Chifforobe for something pretty to wear to work in case she ran into Victor. She pulled out her mother's pink flowered dress and raised it to her nose. Inhaling, she closed her eyes and took in the faint hint of the Rose perfume Carolyn wore.

With a stitch here and there, she adjusted the hand me downs until they fit her slim body. "Oh, Mama, I want this boy to like me. He's not like anyone I've ever met. He fills the room with his presence and leaves me gasping for air. I wish I had money, I'd go to the drug store for lunch so I could see him again."

She sat at her dressing table and combed her hair. She decided instead of pulling it into a bun she would wear it down. In order to keep it out of her eyes, she placed the hair on top of her head in a clip. Friday meant more customers and no boxes to unpack.

She left the boarding house and walked to Main Street. Her daddy had been sober for the last few days. He and Ella were getting along quite well. They gathered in the parlor or on the porch every night. Ella brought out boxes of pictures, some of them of Carolyn. Dottie couldn't believe how much she favored her mother. Ella and Avery talked about their childhood and how the town had changed since they were young. The pictures of Ella showed a pretty girl; she looked nothing like that now. She appeared older than her years. The hard work and disappointments were etched into the lines of her face. Dottie didn't want to be an old maid. She wanted a husband who didn't drink, someone who loved her, as much as her mama loved her daddy.

She remembered asking her mama how she could stay with her daddy especially when he drank. Carolyn told her, "*Dottie, if you remember anything I've taught you, remember this. The Bible says in First Corinthians, Chapter thirteen that love bears all things, believes all things, hopes all things, endures all things. This is the definition of unconditional love.*"

Could she love anyone that much?

A few boys showed her attention. Some even told her they loved her, but they all left. Did any man have deep feelings for their wife? Her daddy wasn't faithful, she'd seen him tomcatting with her own eyes. She wanted unconditional love. She would find it, if she had to leave this town and her daddy behind.

She arrived at work a few minutes early. "Good morning, Mr. Murphy."

"Morning Dottie. I want you to clean the glass cabinets today when you aren't waiting on customers."

She grabbed the broom. "I will, but first I'm going to sweep the sidewalk." She stepped out the door and cleaned the area in front of the store. She peeped across the street. Victor turned the closed sign to open. She stopped and stared.

He opened the door and walked out on the sidewalk. "Good Morning, Miss Lester."

Dottie smiled. "Mr. Douglas." She continued to sweep watching the handsome man out of the corner of her eye until he went in the Drug Store.

Chapter Six

The Douglas family filled every inch of Jacob's 1932 Buick. Hattie rode in the back with the girls to give Victor more room in the front.

Jacob turned the car into the Saplingville Baptist Church parking lot and found a place close to the cemetery. Lisbeth jumped out and ran into the church to practice her offertory song before the service. They entered the church, and sat on their pew. Everyone in the church had a place to sit. Their space had been passed from his grandparents on his mother's side. The music leader announced the first hymn as 'Jesus Saves,' page 97. Lisbeth played the introduction and the singing of the congregation raised the rafters of the church.

He didn't open the hymnbook; the words were engraved on his heart. His baritone voice rose above the others. After the singing of the hymn, Pastor Lowe started the service with a prayer. Victor glanced around the church. Dottie and Ella Simons entered taking their seat on the back row. He took note of Dottie's features. She had a full face, a small nose, big teeth that broke into a huge smile and the prettiest brown eyes he'd ever seen. He wouldn't classify her as beautiful but she was very pretty. He had noticed something else about her when he met her at Murphy's. She couldn't be much older than Ruth Ann, but she had confidence, and put everything into her work. He couldn't wait for the service to end so they could talk.

He listened as Pastor Lowe preached his favorite sermon about sinners, how they needed to repent of their ways and be born again. The preacher slammed his hand on the pulpit and knocked his water glass over. He got a loud Amen from the men, and Praise the Lord from the women. The altar call brought three men and one lady for prayer. Most of the congregation left their seats to pray over them.

When everyone returned to their pews, Pastor Lowe yelled, as he walked toward the door, "There is shouting all over Heaven today because these four people have been born again."

The congregation sang 'Praise Him! Praise Him!' as Pastor Lowe stood at the door waiting to greet his parishioners. Victor waited patiently for the song to be over while looking at the pretty girl. He walked out of his pew and got caught in the crowd. By the time he got to the door, Dottie and Miss Simons were walking away from the church.

He and his family waited at the car for Lisbeth. She played the postlude while everyone exited the church. Ruth Ann sat behind Jacob. When Lisbeth arrived, he helped her and his mother into the back seat and settled into the passenger seat. "Pa, can you drop me by the house so I can get my car."

"Why do you need it?"

"Frankie and I are working on the Jenny this afternoon. I told him I'd pick him up."

"Sure, no problem."

He got out of the car and helped his mother get in the front seat. "See y'all in a few minutes."

He changed out of his Sunday suit and put a short sleeved shirt over his t-shirt and denim pants. He drove by the boarding house which became either habit or desperation. He didn't see Dottie outside, so he turned his car in the direction of the shanty town.

Frankie waited in front of his house. He stopped the car so his friend could jump in. "I watched for you at church today."

Frankie closed the car door and rolled down his window. "Well, I didn't make it, did I?"

"You missed a good sermon, Pastor Lowe preached on sinners and repenting, four people were born again." Victor eased off the clutch, the car lurched forward.

"Well, if I'd come, he would've preached on back slid sinners. That's what he told me I was last time he came to visit." Frankie muttered, "Is Ruthie coming today?"

"She'll be there, but don't start anything. I want to eat and get to work on the plane so we can fly this afternoon before dark sets in." He turned on the highway and shifted to the last gear driving as fast as the old car would go.

"I'll be nice if she is." Frankie hesitated. "You gonna let me fly today?"

He contemplated him and rolled his eyes. "What do you think?"

"I thought I'd give it a try."

Victor loved the drive out of town to his uncle's house. The farmers had lots of land so you didn't see a house for miles. The huge pastures were filled with cows grazing or horses resting under large oak trees. Many times he would wait for a stray cow blocking the road but today all was clear. They arrived at the white farmhouse and parked in the shaded driveway beside Jacob's car. The old house had been built onto at an angle. It appeared to be two houses joined together, one behind the other, both with a wide porch running along the front of the house. He'd been baffled by that since he became old enough to understand architecture. He noticed the second floor of the old part had a window on the side. If a room had been added beside the old part of the house, they would lose the window. In the Georgia heat, you needed windows for cross ventilation.

Aunt Delores met them at the door. "Hi boys, glad you can join us. Go wash your hands, everyone's at the table."

Victor and Frankie found their places.

Uncle Walter nodded to them. "Let's bow our heads, I'll say grace." Walter said Amen and smiled at his family. "Everything we have to eat today is from the farm, from the chicken to the vegetables. God is good to us."

He watched as Frankie dove into the bowls as they were passed. Frankie didn't get to eat like this, unless invited. Aunt Delores advised them not to eat too much, she had a fresh blackberry cobbler for dessert. The women talked about who came to church and the situation with the WMU fund raiser. The men talked about farming, President Roosevelt, and the New Deal. He couldn't get his mind off Dottie. She looked pretty today in her yellow flowered dress and hat. After blackberry cobbler and more sweet tea, he and Frankie said their goodbyes.

They walked to the car and took off their shirts.

"No sense ruining good clothes." Victor said as he carefully placed it on the back of his seat.

Frankie agreed. "You're right. I've got lots of good shirts with grease stains that won't come out. Boy what a meal, your Aunt Delores is the best cook in the world."

"She is, glad you could join us."

"What do we need to do today?"

Victor turned toward the barn. "We need to grease the valve gear, before we start out. I don't like to get beyond forty hours. I left some oil in the barn, and we need the gas can."

Frankie walked ahead, turned, and faced him. "The barnstormer team always went fifty hours before greasing."

He kept walking. "I'd rather be safe than sorry. It's my military training."

They walked into the barn and let their eyes adjust to the dappled light streaming from the open door. Victor stood for a minute taking in the smell of old hay and horse manure. A chicken roosting on a post stood and let out a cackle. He opened the door to the corner closet, grabbed the oil, and handed Frankie the gas can. They headed to the Jenny.

Frankie sat the container next to the bi-plane. "You've been quiet today, must be the girl Ruthie talked about. What's her name?"

"Her name's Dottie Lester, and I saw her first, so don't go gettin' any ideas."

"So, when are you gonna see her?"

"I barely know her."

"Yeah, and usually, you've already made your move by now. Take her to a movie or better yet, take her for a ride in the Jenny."

He didn't want to talk about her, not yet. "I'm working on it."

"Victor, I've figured out how to make money with our...I mean your Jenny. Crop dusting. You can fly and drop the chemicals, I can be the flagman. Of course, if you get tired of flying, you can be the flagman and I'll fly. Walter would hire us, and probably most of the other farmers."

"Frankie, I'm not staying. I sent a letter to Delta Air Lines last week. I'm waiting word for an interview."

Frankie walked in front of Victor and stopped. "Well you finally did it. I'll buy the Jenny back from you, start my own crop dusting business, and take the dame, too."

He ignored him as he climbed on the front wheel. "You gas up and I'll grease the valve gear." He checked the wind sock. "Nice day to fly, no wind, and not a cloud in the sky. Untie her while I finish."

Victor put the oil can next to a tree. They pushed the Jenny out straight on the make shift runway. He climbed into the seat while Frankie spun the propeller through until the engine fired. The valve gears popping reminded him of the sound of the cotton mill spinning thread into cloth—the spark plugs in the eight cylinders sounded just right. He waited for his friend to jump in the front seat. Even though the bi-plane had dual controls, the pilot usually sat in the back, because if only one person flew the weight in the plane balanced.

Victor decided a long time would pass, before Frankie sat in the pilot seat. He took off into the air as the whoosh of wind and noise roused his senses. Flying an airplane thrilled him, from the bombers he flew in practice runs over the Pacific to the little JN-4 Jenny bi-plane. He soared over Uncle Walter's one hundred acres. He watched the ducks wade in the lake and the cows graze in the pasture. He took the plane to five thousand feet and headed west to Lake Harding.

The flight to the Alabama state line took less than an hour. He had plenty of time to get back. Anything over two hours, and he would be looking for a place to land. He loved his time in the air. The engine noise made it impossible to communicate. Occasionally he would fly low enough to see the typical Sunday afternoon sights, people swimming in the creeks, and others riding horses through the fields. If there were no trees, he would fly low enough to wave.

The two hours passed quickly. His uncle waited in his usual spot. Walter loved the bi-plane and enjoyed flying. He didn't go much because Delores didn't want him to fly. Frankie jumped out and helped guide the plane to the little shelter Walter built for them.

After tying down the wheels, his uncle said, "Victor, come by one night next week, I want to talk to you about something."

"I'll come by tomorrow after work." He placed his hat and goggles in the airplane.

Victor and Frankie stopped by the front porch, where Delores shelled a bowl of peas. He gave his aunt a kiss on the cheek. "Thanks for Sunday dinner."

Frankie chimed in, "Yes, thank you, the food was delicious. You're the best cook in the world."

"Thanks, boys. I'm glad you had a safe flight today. Guess we'll see you next week?"

Victor walked down the porch steps. "If the

weather's good."

They were quiet on the drive to shanty town, both in a flight trance. Neither of them wanted to start another work week.

As they arrived at Frankie's house, he urged Victor. "Ask her out."

"I might."

"You ain't getting no younger."

"You ain't neither."

They both laughed. Victor watched as his friend climbed the step to his porch, and opened the front door to his house.

He turned his car toward home. *What did Uncle Walter want to talk about?* Could be about Jacob's health. He didn't need a lecture. His car turned in the direction of the boarding house. Dottie sat on the porch alone. He parked on the street and put on his short sleeved shirt. His palms were sweating as he hurried to fasten the buttons. He got to the bottom and he had a button left over. He had to start over. *Calm down, it's just a girl, jeez.*

He put on his biggest smile as he strolled toward her. "Evening Miss Lester, mind if I join you?"

She stood and walked to the edge of the porch leaning over the rail. "Hello, Mr. Douglas."

He climbed the few steps to the porch. "I wanted to talk to you this morning at church."

She motioned for him to sit. "Ella always cooks Sunday Dinner for the boarders. I told her I'd help."

He sat beside her in the swing. "I had dinner with my family at my Uncle Walter's house, and then I flew my airplane."

Dottie's face lit up. "You have an airplane, here in

Saplingville?"

"I sure do, maybe you'll go for a ride with me."

"I'll have to think about it, I've never flown before." She studied Victor's profile. "Where'd you learn to fly?"

"The United States Army Air Corp." He turned his head and locked his eyes with hers.

"What kind of plane do you have?" Dottie whispered.

"I have a Curtiss JN-4 bi-plane. The plane isn't very big, it has two seats. I bought it from a friend of mine." He stared at her lips imagining how they would taste. "Now tell me about you, how'd you end up in Saplingville?"

"My parents were raised here. Mama died a few months ago, and Daddy said we should move to his hometown." Dottie spoke softly and stared at the floor. "I took a job at Murphy's. He hired me because he knew my grandpa."

He reached over and took her hand, "I'm sorry about your mama, losing her had to be hard for you."

She gazed at Victor's hand covering hers. "Losing Mama's been hard, but Daddy and I will be fine."

Reluctantly he pulled his hand away. He could smell her hair. He leaned closer, she smelled clean like clothes hanging on a line. He wanted to put his arm around her and kiss her lips. It had been awhile since he had been with a girl and he wanted to do some delicious things to Miss Dottie Lester. He'd be gone soon but what would be wrong in having a little fun before he left. After all, she was new in town, and needed to make friends.

Victor's jeans grew tight, he took a breath, thinking

of anything other than the girl on the swing beside him. "My parents were born and raised here. Ma said she remembers your parents. Do you have more family in town?"

"No, Mama's sister lives in Macon. She wants me to move there. I'm considering it, if things don't work out here."

"Well I hope things work out for you. I'd like to see more of you."

She stared at the freshly painted floor. "That would be nice." She raised her head and almost hit him in the face. "How about you, do you have brothers and sisters?"

He rested in the swing. "I have two sisters, Ruth Ann's sixteen and Lisbeth's fourteen. Lisbeth plays the piano at church."

"Oh, that's your sister? She's great."

"Both of my siblings like to be in the spotlight. Ruth Ann wants to be an actress but Lisbeth's content to play her music."

"They both sound like very smart girls."

"Yes, they are. I have a good family."

Dottie lowered her eyes. "Don't ever take them for granted. I only got to be with Mama for nineteen years."

Victor brushed her hair from her face. Their eyes locked. "I'm sorry, what you've been through isn't fair." He took her hand and kissed it.

She could only whisper. "Any other family in town?"

"Yes, my Uncle Walter and Aunt Delores live on a farm outside of town. I keep my bi-plane there."

Dottie cleared her throat. "I never knew anyone

who had an airplane. How exciting."

"Flying's exciting, I can't wait to take you."

"Isn't it scary? I mean how does the plane get off the ground?" She shifted in her seat and Victor steadied the swing.

"Everyone asks the same question." He pushed with his feet as the swing swayed under his weight.

"What kind of plane did you fly in the service?"

He couldn't remember a time when flying hadn't been a part of his life. "I took flying lessons before I went in. The USAAC started me in bi-planes, then bombers."

"Did you bomb anything?"

"No, fortunately we didn't."

"You're lucky. Daddy fought in World War One. Mama said the war changed him. It's one reason he drinks too much. The other reason is he misses her."

"Getting over a loss takes time."

"Yes, that's what Ella said."

He rose from his chair and pulled her up. He resisted the urge to pull her closer. "I enjoyed our talk. I'll see you around, Miss Lester."

Dottie's body swayed and she stiffened her legs to steady herself. "I look forward to it."

Victor drove home slowly. He liked Dottie Lester, she stirred a fire he hadn't experienced in quite some time. Boredom with this town and his life flooded his bones. She was pretty and all woman but she was also innocent. The girls he met in California were loose and available especially to a man in uniform. They were looking for a good time and he gave it to them.

He would have to tread carefully with this girl. He wouldn't be able to live with himself if he took advantage of her innocence and left her to face town gossip. What if she got pregnant? He always took precautions but sometimes it did happen. That's the last thing he needed.

He parked his car and went inside. Everyone sat in the living room listening to the radio. "I'm home."

Hattie stood and hugged her son. "Did you have fun flying?"

"Frankie and I worked on the plane and had a good flight to Alabama and back."

Jacob adjusted the sound on the radio. The voice of President Roosevelt and his Fireside Chat filled the room. "I'm going to bed, see y'all in the morning."

He couldn't go to sleep. The way Mr. Lester took advantage of Dottie for financial support made him furious. A father should take care of his daughter, especially when the daughter grew up taking care of her sick mother. She deserved more. He had a strong urge to protect her, and make her life better. He would spend as much time as he could with Dottie Lester before he left town.

Chapter Seven

Dottie sat in the parlor reading *Tobacco Road* by Erskine Caldwell. She had a quiet day at work. Too quiet because she'd only seen Victor once as he walked home with his father after closing the Drug Store. She hadn't thought of anything but him since he'd stopped by last night. A knock on the door brought her out of her daze.

Pastor Lowe stood on the porch, smiling. "Hello, young lady. May I come in?"

"Yes sir, come in." Dottie pushed the screen door open and stepped aside.

"I came to see you and Miss Simons, and Mr. Lester, if he's home."

"Sure. Please, sit and I'll get them."

She found Ella in the kitchen. She put her hand to her mouth and whispered, "Pastor Lowe's here for a visit. I'm going to get Daddy."

She tiptoed to her father's room and peeked inside. Avery sat in a chair staring out the window. She walked in the room and closed the door. "Pastor Lowe's here for a visit. He wants to see you."

Avery gritted his teeth and sneered. "Well, I don't want to see him."

"Please, Daddy. He asked to see you."

Avery stood and steadied himself before he walked to the door. "I'm doing this for you."

She and her daddy sat on the sofa as Ella handed out glasses of iced tea.

Pastor Lowe took a sip. "Dottie, I'm glad you and Miss Simons came to church Sunday. Mr. Lester, why didn't you come with them?"

Avery placed his tea glass on the side table. "I slept late, I'll try to come next Sunday."

Pastor Lowe took another swig of tea. "I heard about Carolyn, I'm sorry for your loss."

Dottie wiped a tear from her face. She thought about her mama all the time but she didn't cry unless someone brought the subject up.

Avery fixed his gaze on Pastor Lowe. "Thank you for your concern. I still have my baby girl to take care of." Avery nodded toward Dottie.

She stared at Ella. She wanted to scream and say, who's taking care of who? She put her hands in her lap, fixed her gaze on the floor, and counted the number of pink and yellow roses on the linoleum rug.

Pastor Lowe leaned forward in his chair. "Avery, I want to leave this scripture with you, and then pray for you. Acts eight, verse twenty-two says, 'Repent therefore of this your wickedness, and pray God if perhaps the thought of your heart may be forgiven you'."

The preacher prayed for peace, and healing in Dottie and Avery's hearts over the loss of Carolyn. He prayed Avery would be strong, and overcome the demons in his life. He didn't say what the demons were, but she figured if Pastor Lowe knew, then the whole town did too.

Chapter Eight

Victor parked his old car behind Uncle Walter's dark green 1930 Ford truck. It appeared brand new despite being used for hauling vegetables to market and farm chores. Walter waxed the truck and varnished the wood around the bed. He admired his uncle's work ethic, never one to sit and twiddle his thumbs, he stayed busy year round.

Walter relaxed in a rocker and waved.

"Uncle Walter, how you doin'?" Before stepping to the porch, he gave the old mixed breed dog's head a gentle scratch.

The old man moved the rocking chairs close together. "Glad you could come. Take a seat."

Aunt Delores pushed open the screen door and handed them glasses of sweet tea. "Victor, it's good to see you. How's everyone?"

He took the cold glass. "Everyone's fine. I hope you aren't working too much. Summer's your busy time with your vegetable garden and canning."

Delores turned to go in the house. "I am very busy but I love it and the vegetables are so good in the winter time. I'm going to leave you two, it's time for the Eddie Cantor Show."

Victor started rocking in the old chair. "Uncle Walter, what did you want to see me about? You didn't invite me out here to drink tea with you."

"You're right." Walter took a sip of iced tea and turned all of his attention to his nephew. "The misses and I've been talking. We're not gettin' any younger. We need to make some plans for the future. God didn't bless us with children, but He blessed us with a fine nephew. We're making a will. We want to leave our farm to you, when we're gone."

He stood and locked eyes with his uncle. "No need to talk like that, you've got lots of years ahead."

"Hear me out on this. I've seen it happen many times. A man dies with no heirs. The state takes the house and land. I've worked too hard all these years, for this to happen to us. This land's been in the Andrews' family for two generations. Hattie married Jacob, and moved to town, didn't want anything to do with the farm land. Even though you love the outdoors, you're not a farmer and being cooped up in a drug store for the rest of your life isn't what you want."

Victor stared at a cat walking through the yard. "Yes, I feel guilty."

"Don't. You're not like your father. Lisbeth would come closer to taking over the family business. She's quiet and studious like Jacob. You're like the Andrews side of the family, we like the open spaces, being outside, working outside."

"You're right, I don't care a thing about farming. Why leave the land to me?"

"Sit, I'll tell you."

He turned the rocker to face his uncle and sipped his tea. He couldn't believe their conversation about dying and a will.

Walter continued, "I've seen a lot of changes in the last thirty years. We had no electricity, no telephone, no indoor plumbing, and we drove a horse and wagon to town. Now I've got a nice Ford truck and an airplane sittin' on my land. Transportation's the future. My proposition is this. I'll deed you forty acres now. There's enough of the forty acres cleared off so you can open a small airport. When you get money, clear off more land. Hire Frankie, he'd be good help. We need someone to crop dust."

Victor laughed. "Yes, Frankie's trying to talk me into converting the Jenny."

He walked to the porch rail and turned. "Uncle Walter, I'm honored, but I sent an application for a commercial pilot job in Atlanta."

Walter stood and put his hand on Victor's arm. "The land will always be yours, and when we're gone you'll inherit the entire farm. If you change your mind, the forty acres is yours now."

He backed his car out of the driveway and headed toward town. It was a generous offer. His own airport sounded great, but there were many things to consider. What if no one used the airport? How many years would be required for an airport in this part of the country to be successful? Where would he get the money to buy more planes, much less build a tower, and the covered hangers he needed?

His mind raced with excitement about the prospect. One thought nagged him, he would be more of an administrator than a pilot. He could give flying lessons, but he wouldn't be able to fly large commercial airplanes around the country. He drove home thinking and weighing his options. Two things tugged at him to stay, Dottie and Uncle Walter's proposal. The urge to leave and fly commercial airliners dominated.

Chapter Nine

Victor stood on the sidewalk with his leg bent behind him and his foot on the wall of the column when Dottie came out of the Five and Dime. He waited for ten minutes for her to get off work. He shouldn't, but he had to find out more about this bewitching woman. She exited the store staring at the sidewalk.

He stepped in front of her. "Miss Lester, how are you today? Mind if I walk you home?"

She jumped, startled. "I'm good. Sure, if you want to."

"Sorry, I didn't mean to scare you." He studied her face. "I hope you had a good day, mine was the usual."

"What do you do at the drug store?" She fell into step with him.

"I keep the books, order supplies, cook lunch at the grill, and keep the place clean. My father dispenses medicine. He did everything except cook and clean but his health's not good. I returned to help him, until he can find someone. He's not looking for anyone to replace me. I'm to blame, because I fell into the daily grind." They stopped and waited for a car to go by. He put his hand on her arm and guided her across the street.

"Sounds like you do most of the work."

"Well, I'm younger and healthy. I want to take as much stress off him as I can. I'm happy to help." He held onto her arm until they were safely on the sidewalk.

"You're a good son."

"Not as good as I should be. We had a heated discussion last week. I told him I would leave soon. The conversation didn't go well. If my sisters were already out of the house, my mother could help, but he says she's too scatter brained. He's probably right. She's a good person and means well, but her mind's in the clouds most of the time. They say opposites attract and boy, are they opposites." His hand brushed against Dottie's. He reached for it and their fingers locked together. "My father's very smart and reads all the time. His customers ask his advice about medications before they go to their doctor."

"Where are you going?"

He heard disappointment in her voice. "I applied for a job with Delta Air Lines in Atlanta, to be a commercial airline pilot."

"You must love to fly."

"I do. There's nothing like it. Being in the air changes your perspective on everything. My Uncle Walter told me when you have a problem pretend you're flying. When you look down over the problem, it won't seem so big and you'll probably find an answer. He's right. When you go flying with me you'll see what I mean."

Dottie observed the heavens. "What can you see when you're in the sky?"

He stopped and followed her gaze. "Depends on how high you are. If you're taking off or landing you can see the land and houses very clear. The higher you go, the smaller things become. Once you're in the clouds, that's all you can see."

They continued walking. "How does it feel, floating in the clouds?"

"Peaceful, and very relaxing."

"Are you ever afraid?"

"Flying's dangerous, I'll admit." A woman with a baby carriage walked toward them. They stopped and let her pass.

"But yet you still fly. Why?"

"For me it's a siren song. The sky beckons, and I follow."

"Do all pilots feel the same?"

"I believe so."

He walked her to the front door of the boarding house. The walk home had been quick. *I monopolized the conversation. I didn't find out anything about her.*

Victor took both of her hands in his. "How about going to the picture show with me? I can pick you up at seven." He heard Mr. Lester yell, "Baby, girl is that you? Come in the house."

She peered through the screen door. "How about another day? I'm tired, and don't feel like going out, but thanks for walking me home."

Victor pressed his lips together. "You betcha."

He would love to wring Avery Lester's neck. He could tell by his slurring words, he was as drunk as Cooter Brown. A sweet, kind, smart girl like her deserved more. He might be leaving in a month or two but he would take every opportunity to make Dottie's life better until then.

Chapter Ten

Dottie walked to the parlor and found her daddy slumped in a chair. "You told me you were going to hunt for a job today."

"I looked but didn't find none."

"You certainly found this." She grabbed the bottle of bourbon, and headed to the bathroom sink.

Avery shot out of his chair. Unable to grab the bottle, he fell and hit his head on the door jamb.

She poured the amber liquid down the bathroom sink.

Avery slid to the floor swearing. He rubbed his head with one hand, and pulled her to the floor with the other. "Your mama would have never done that to me."

Dottie stood. She scrutinized her father, stepped over him and crossed the room to the door. Hesitating, she turned. "I'm sorry, Daddy. I can't do this anymore."

She left him on the floor and walked to the kitchen. She sat at the table, while Ella poured her a glass of tea and fixed her a sandwich. Dottie could see the mantel clock in the parlor. She heard the ticking sound and stared at it. The hands of the clock stood still, like her life.

Ella finished cleaning the counter and sat. "I'm not sure if he went on a job search today or if he only left the house to buy his bourbon."

Dottie put down her sandwich. "How long was he

gone?"

"He left at nine this morning. He came home about one. He wasn't drunk when he got here, just sad and depressed."

"He's really mad. I poured what was left in the bottle down the sink. I told him, I can't do this anymore. All I do is go to work every day, come in at night, and take care of him. He doesn't care about me or my feelings, he never asks about my job, or how my day went. He doesn't care about anyone but himself."

Ella clasped Dottie's hands. "Things'll get better, I promise. There's always dark before dawn. I noticed Victor walked you home today."

"He wanted me to go to the picture show. When he asked me, Daddy heard me and yelled for me to come in the house. He won't ask me again, I'm sure."

"I bet he will."

"Thanks for the sandwich." Dottie washed her plate and glass and placed them in the drainer. "I'm going to my room."

Dottie held on to the bannister letting it pull her up the stairs. She faced the rocker toward the window and stared into the darkness. Thoughts of her daddy and Victor came so fast she couldn't keep up. Her daddy would never get a job, and the days with the man of her dreams were numbered. The only person she could count on in this world lived in Macon. Aunt Bess' invitation to live with her sounded better every day.

Chapter Eleven

Hattie called everyone to supper. Victor went to the sink to wash his hands. They sat and Hattie blessed the food. He filled his bowl with Beef Stew and passed the large bowl to Ruth Ann.

"Caught a glimpse of you and Dottie today." Ruth Ann spooned stew into her bowl.

"Yes, I walked her home from work. Her mama died a few months ago."

Hattie put her hand to her chest. "Oh, no, Carolyn died, how sad."

Jacob put his spoon in his bowl and studied his son. "Are you sure you want to start a friendship with this girl?"

Hattie straightened in her chair. "She sounds like a sweet girl, what's wrong with him seeing her? We could have her over for supper one night. Victor, you ask her and give me a day's notice so I can set the china out. I remember the last time you brought a girl home for supper. You didn't tell me you invited her. All I'd prepared was vegetable soup and corn bread."

"Ma, she told me, the vegetable soup and corn bread was the best she ever ate."

Hattie asked, "Where did she end up?"

"She got married, and moved away after I went in the service, remember?"

Hattie nodded her head. "I do remember. Her name

was Catherine Sanders. She married your friend Mark Taylor."

"Yes, last I heard they moved to North Carolina." Victor took a bite of biscuit.

They finished their stew, Jacob and Ruth Ann made their way to the parlor.

It was Victor and Lisbeth's night to wash dishes. Hattie helped them clear the table. He washed and his sister dried.

Lisbeth stacked the dishes on the counter. "I don't see what the big deal is. Why should Pa and Ruth Ann care who you date?"

"I agree with you. I don't see what the big deal is either." He let the water out of the sink and rung out the rag.

"Is it because her daddy drinks? Why would you hold something against a person because of what their parents do?"

Victor smiled at his little sister. "You're a smart girl."

Lisbeth blushed. "Thanks."

They walked into the parlor. Jacob sat in his big chair and Hattie in her rocking chair. Victor and Lisbeth sat with Ruth Ann on the sofa. The Rudy Vallée Show came through the radio speakers. Rudy sang 'Life Is Just a Bowl of Cherries' with Ethel Merman. He excused himself before the show was over, and headed upstairs to bed.

As he climbed the stairs, he heard his ma, Ruth Ann and Lisbeth make plans to go to Murphy's Five and Dime tomorrow. He smiled, why did it take them so long?

Chapter Twelve

Dottie watched Hattie, Ruth Ann and Lisbeth enter the store. *No need to get nervous, treat them like other customers.* "May I help you with something?"

"We're just looking dear," Hattie replied.

Lisbeth searched through the stationery.

"We got those in yesterday." Dottie moved closer.

Lisbeth pulled the pink paper with three black cats, one playing saxophone, one fiddle and the other guitar with musical notes along the top of the sheets out of the display. "I love this."

"It's called Jazz Cats." She straightened the pens and pencils on a nearby rack.

Lisbeth took note of the other writing material. "I love Jazz music, but I mostly practice classical and sacred. Sometimes, my teacher buys me jazz pieces."

Dottie chose a dark blue Parker Vacuum Filler Ink Pen. "This came in yesterday."

"It's a good pen, I have one at home."

She put it on the display. "I enjoy hearing you play at church, you're very good."

"Thank you."

Lisbeth turned her attention to her mother and Ruth Ann. "Ma, can I get some stationery? They have one with Jazz Cats on the top of the page."

Hattie smiled. "Sure, honey."

They walked to the cash register counter, where

Ruth Ann waited with her red nail polish.

Hattie pulled out her money, to pay for her daughter's things. "Victor's told us about you and we wanted to come by and meet you personally and say hello."

Ruth Ann glared. "Is it true your daddy's the town drunk?"

Hattie's hand flew to her throat. "For goodness sake, he isn't, and this is not polite conversation for a lady."

Ruth Ann said under her breath. "I'm not a lady. She isn't either."

Hattie put her arms around her daughter's shoulders and headed to the front door. She turned and smiled at Dottie. "I am so sorry, I don't know what got into Ruth Ann. It was nice to meet you. We look forward to seeing you at church Sunday."

She forced a smile but her lips wouldn't cooperate. "Nice to meet you too."

"Ruth Ann Douglas that's the most hateful thing you've ever done. Your behavior is unacceptable. Don't ever do anything like that again, you hear me?" Dottie heard Hattie say to her daughter as they exited the store.

She concentrated on her work, but Ruth Ann's words rang in her ears. Everyone in town recognized Avery as the town drunk. Memories of her mama, and the life Carolyn had with him spurred her to take control. She would not be pushed around by her daddy, and people like Ruth Ann. She'd fulfill her promise and see her daddy settled with a job before she left, then, Macon would be her home.

When Dottie clocked out, Victor stood outside the store.

"I hear you met some of my family today." He gave her a questioning smile.

She grinned. "Yep, they came in the store to check me out."

"Well, do I need to apologize or did they behave?" They walked by Price's Jewelry Store and crossed the street.

"Everyone except Ruth Ann."

He let out a belly laugh. "Sounds like her, don't pay her any attention."

"You're right about Lisbeth. She's sweet and polite, and Mrs. Douglas is delightful."

"Yes, my mother is fun loving and impulsive. Total opposite from my father but their differences complement each other."

"Mama was good for Daddy. The sad part is I really don't know him." Her voice faded to a whisper. "If he's sober, he's looking for his next drink."

"I'm sorry, it must be hard for you." He reached for Dottie's hand.

"I'm realizing I can't save him. He has to want to be rescued." The worry about her father faded as she focused on the man beside her.

"Have you thought any more about flying?"

She studied the sky before answering. "Yes, I want to."

"Sunday's a date then, I can't wait for you to see the world from five thousand feet."

"Five thousand feet?"

"Yes, that's about as high as we fly in the Jenny."

"Why did you name your plane Jenny?"

Victor laughed. "The real name of the airplane is Curtiss JN-4. They were popular during the barnstorming days and the name was shortened to Jenny." He pulled her toward him as two little boys ran past.

They continued to walk with his arm around her waist. "The barnstormers put on a show in Macon. When I was fourteen, I spent the summer with Aunt Bess. They were at Miller Field. I'll never forget it. Most of the time, I couldn't watch. The plane started going in a circle in the air, I thought they were going to crash. After the plane did loops and barrel rolls it landed and another crew went up. A man danced on the top wing of the plane."

"My friend, Frankie worked as a barnstormer."

"Did he walk on the wings?"

He guided her across the street. "No, he was a pilot…the best they had. He flew the airplane while the wing walkers did their tricks. He won trophies for his aerobatics."

"After the show, they took people for rides, but we didn't go. How high did you fly in the bombers?"

"The ceiling, or the highest you could fly was close to thirteen thousand feet but we usually only got as high as eleven or twelve thousand."

She loved his confidence. She could tell by their conversation, he took his flying seriously. He had to be a great pilot. "Well, I can't wait to fly."

They slowed their gait when the boarding house came into view. "Good, you'll be the first girl I've taken for an airplane ride. I promise I won't do any tricks and scare you."

"It's hard to believe I'm the first girl. I'm honored."

He took her hand as they climbed the stairs to the

porch. "Good, I'll see you Sunday. Oh, and wear a skirt that isn't tight or short. You'll have to climb into the plane."

Victor left her at her front door and headed home. He hadn't been this excited about a date, in a long time.

Chapter Thirteen

Avery took a plate of bacon, eggs and toast from Ella and sat at the table. "I have a job interview Monday."

Dottie folded her hands together and put them under her chin. "Oh, Daddy, that's great. Who's it with?"

Avery sprinkled salt and pepper on his egg. "Bartholomew's Auto Sales. They need a car salesman."

"I hope you get it."

Ella placed her plate on the table. "I do, too."

After supper, the three sat together on the porch greeting the boarders as they came home. Her feet hadn't touched the ground since she agreed to a date with Victor.

Avery watched his daughter. "You seem happy tonight."

Dottie smiled. "I'm thrilled about your job interview."

"Is that it? I noticed some boy coming around a lot. Who is he?"

"Victor Douglas, he works with his father at Douglas Drug Store." She didn't mention their date. She would tell him later, he would worry about her flying in an airplane. She didn't want to take anything from his excitement about his job interview.

Dottie slept late Saturday morning. By the time she got up, Avery was nowhere to be seen. She spent the day washing their clothes in the bathtub and hanging them on the line in the back yard. In the late afternoon, she searched through Sunday dresses to find something appropriate for church and flying. She heard a commotion and ran downstairs as Avery stumbled in the front door. Drunk again.

"Baby girl, where are you baby girl?"

"Daddy, what have you done? You promised me you wouldn't do this again." She steadied him.

"Do what? I didn't do anything, where's Ella? Ella?" He grabbed her arm, she braced herself grabbing the chair.

"She's not here."

Avery headed for the bathroom. He cursed between heaves. She sat on his bed and started crying. She couldn't leave him tomorrow morning, she had to get him ready for Monday. Victor wouldn't ask her out again. The certainty rested heavy on her heart.

He came out of the bathroom and glared at her. "What's the matter with you?"

Dottie wiped the tears from her cheek and shuffled to the bathroom. She wet a rag and walked into her daddy's room. "Lie down and put this on your forehead. I'll get you an aspirin."

Avery kicked the chair, it hit the wall. "Did you hear what I asked you?" He lunged toward her. "What you crying for, little girl?"

She backed out of the room stumbling over the broken furniture. She slammed the door and held the doorknob as Avery pounded. She hoped he wouldn't try to open it. She heard him stumble to the bed. She didn't relax until the bed creaked with his weight. She walked upstairs feeling her way in the dark. She entered her room moving her hand through the air until she felt the light string. The bare bulb cast a spotlight over the carefully laid out clothes covering the bed. She grabbed them and threw the dress, gloves and hat in the Chifforobe.

Chapter Fourteen

Sunday morning Victor whistled as he got dressed for church. He put a change of clothes in a paper bag and walked into the kitchen. "Morning, Ma."

Hattie handed him a cup of coffee. "You look cheerful."

"I have a date after church. I'm taking Dottie flying."

"Has she flown before?"

"No, but she's excited about it. If she likes it, we'll fly to the Alabama line and back."

Hattie stirred the grits. "If she doesn't?"

"I'll turn the plane and head to the runway." He helped his mother by putting butter on bread for toast.

"Well, don't be disappointed. Not everyone loves to fly like you and Frankie." Hattie took the sausage out of the iron skillet and poured beaten eggs in.

"I know, Ma." He walked to the stairs. "Time for breakfast."

The family gathered at the table. Hattie passed the sausage and eggs. "What's everyone's plans for today? Will you be here for lunch?"

"I'm going to a movie with friends but I'll be here for lunch." Ruth Ann smeared muscadine jelly on her toast.

Hattie poured coffee in Jacob's cup. "Did you ask your sister if she wanted to go with you?"

Lisbeth shook her head. "I don't care anything about it."

"I won't be here, we'll grab a hamburger before we fly." He walked to the sink with his plate. "I'll clean, Ma, you finish getting ready."

Victor met his family at church where they sat in their usual pew. He watched for Dottie through the entire service. He headed to the boarding house and knocked on the door, no one came. He walked to his car and stared at the top floor windows. The lace curtain moved aside and slowly settled in place. He drove through the streets of town. Did he say something to upset her? Could she be sick? He'd never been stood up before. He opened the back door and walked into the kitchen. The family sat at the table eating lunch. He took a plate and spoon and sat.

Hattie passed the bowl of soup and plate of biscuits. "I thought you had a date."

Victor spooned vegetable soup into his bowl. "I did too. We must have got our dates crossed. She wasn't home." He glared at Ruth Ann. She had a smirk on her face. He stared at her for a few seconds. *What's she's up to?*

"That must be it." Hattie gave her son a big smile.

"Told you not to get mixed up with her." Ruth Ann reached for a biscuit.

Hattie put her spoon down. "If you can't say anything nice about anyone…"

"Yeah, just don't say anything, I know." Ruth Ann rolled her eyes and took a bite of the biscuit.

Victor joined his father in the parlor while the girls cleaned the dishes. They read through the Sunday paper, exchanging sections without a word. A knock on the front door and people talking drew his attention.

Ruth Ann ran down the stairs to the front door. "Come in."

"Are you ready to go?" a strange male voice asked his sister.

"Yes. Victor's here." Ruth Ann lowered her voice.

"He is?" A female voice, Victor identified as Anna.

Victor peered over the top of his paper as his sister pushed Anna into the parlor.

"Harold, come on, I'll introduce you." Ruth Ann said as she pulled on the boy's hand.

"Victor, you remember Anna."

He lowered the paper and nodded. "Yes, Anna, how are you?"

Ruth Ann continued. "And this is Harold."

Victor stood and shook Harold's hand. "Harold, nice to meet you."

Jacob put the paper down and nodded. "Harold."

Ruth Ann grabbed Harold's arm. "Want to go to the picture show with us this afternoon?"

He couldn't have what he wanted. A trip to the theater would be better than staying cooped up in the house. "Yeah, I'll go with you."

"It's a nice day, let's walk," Ruth Ann said as they gathered on the front porch.

The foursome strolled on the side street until they arrived at the wide sidewalks on the main thoroughfare to town. Victor walked behind them. They turned down the road leading to the boarding house. He walked faster and caught his sister, "This isn't the way to the movie theater."

"I'm taking a shortcut."

By this time Anna walked by his side. Harold

walked with Ruth Ann, as if they were a foursome out for a Sunday double date. He distanced himself but Harold started talking about airplanes and Victor got lost in the conversation.

Chapter Fifteen

Dottie put on her thin cotton gown and slid a chair to the window hoping to catch a night breeze. Disappointment ran through her veins as the sweltering heat settled on her skin. She wiped tears from her eyes with one of her mother's handkerchiefs. Could she tell Victor she had to stay home and babysit her daddy? The trouble with her father was hers alone to fix. After midnight, she tossed and turned until sleep came.

She'd left the shade up and the sun bore into her little room. She opened her eyes, squinted, and lifted her hand to shield the light as she walked to the window to pull it down. She wet a rag with cool water and placed it over her swollen and burning eyes.

She dressed and went to check on her daddy. She opened the door and peeked in. Avery didn't move, she pulled the sheet over him and backed out of the room. She went to the kitchen and found Ella drinking coffee. "Good Morning, aren't you going to church?"

She stood to get a cup of coffee for Dottie. "I didn't hear you stirring this morning so I figured you were sleeping in. I just got up myself."

She took the cup, splashed milk in and stirred. "Daddy came in drunk, I didn't get to sleep until late. Can I fix him some chicken soup this morning? I've got to get him ready for his job interview."

"Sure honey, anything you need."

Dottie went to work on her chicken soup. She heard the bells from the First United Methodist Church ring in the hour of eleven. She pictured Victor sitting in the pew with his family at the Baptist Church.

She knocked on her daddy's door. "Are you awake?"

He opened the door and struggled with the buttons on his shirt. "I want to apologize for anything I did last night. When I got up this morning, I found the broken chair and the hole in the wall. I didn't hurt you, did I?"

She took over the job of dressing him, smoothing the collar.

Avery wiped a tear from her face. "I'm so sorry. I didn't know what I was doing."

A flood gate opened, she sobbed on her daddy's shoulder. When there were no more tears, she straightened and pulled away. "I made you some chicken soup, it's in the kitchen when you're ready. Help yourself."

"Thanks. Are you going anywhere today?"

"No, I'll be here all day. What do you need?" Dottie contemplated her answer.

"Will you help me pick out my clothes for tomorrow?"

****

Later that afternoon, Avery laughed and talked with Dottie and Ella like nothing ever happened. He promised Ella he'd fix the hole in the wall.

She helped her father rummage through clothes in his Chifforobe. She took a couple of ties to the window with his suit coat so she could see the colors in a better light. Several people walked down the side walk. She adjusted her sight through the screen. It couldn't be.

Victor walked beside a young pretty girl. Ruth Ann walked with a boy who had his arm around her waist. It was as if someone sucker punched her in the stomach, the air gone from her lungs. She sat in the nearest chair, and took a deep breath.

Avery studied her. "Is something the matter?"

She closed her eyes and willed the tears away. "No, nothing's the matter. I'm a little tired today's, all."

Avery took the ties and coat. "My fault. I promise, I'm trying to do better, and I will. Give me a little time, okay, baby girl."

She stood. "Sure, Daddy. The blue tie works best with the suit."

Dottie went to her room and closed the door. She prayed her daddy's job would work out. She wasn't staying in Saplingville any longer than she had to.

****

The next day at work, Dottie assembled a tea cup and saucer display in the window when Ruth Ann and Anna came in the store. "May I help you with anything?"

The girls laughed and whispered to each other. Ruth Ann wouldn't make eye contact. "No, thank you."

They walked through the store, until they got close enough for Dottie to hear them.

Ruth Ann told Anna, "Victor said he likes you. He's going to ask you out again. We had lots of fun yesterday, didn't we?"

Anna nodded. "I certainly did, Victor's such a gentleman, opening the door, and holding my hand."

The girls started giggling. They left the store without buying anything. Mr. Murphy walked to the front of the store. "Those two girls didn't buy anything, what did they want? Did you try to help them?"

"Yes sir, I asked if they needed any help. They ignored me and walked around the store talking to each other."

Dottie continued setting the cups out and almost dropped one. Her heart pounded against her chest. She didn't need this. Why should she care what Victor did, or who he did it with? She hoped she would see him this afternoon. She would tell him exactly what she thought of him, and his sister.

****

Victor waited for Dottie after work. "Mind if I walk you home?"

She stared straight ahead. "It's a free country."

"Is everything okay? I worried about you, when you didn't come to church yesterday."

Dottie crossed her arms. "I saw you with your girlfriend."

His mind raced. *Girlfriend, what is she talking about?* "I don't have a girlfriend." He remembered his trip to the picture show with his sister. "Oh, I spent the afternoon with my sister and her friends at the theater." She unfolded her arms and glared. "Well, Ruth Ann and your girlfriend came in the store today. They made sure I heard them talking about your date. Your sister said you told her, you're going to ask the girl out again."

"I didn't ask her out in the first place. Anna's too young, and she's Ruth Ann's friend. She has a crush on me, but I'm not interested in her. I'm interested in you, and I didn't like being stood up yesterday. What happened?"

Dottie stopped walking, and took a deep breath.

He cupped her face in his hands. "Are you going to

tell me what happened?"

She closed her eyes. "Daddy got drunk Saturday night. I had to take care of him Sunday and get him ready for his job interview."

"Dottie, I understand. I wish you'd told me. I'm sorry about Ruth Ann and Anna. They had no cause to do that today."

"You can't help what your sister does."

He stopped, grabbed her hands, and faced her. "Let's be honest with each other from now on. Dottie, I like you a lot. I want to get to know you better."

"That would be nice, Victor. I'd like to get to know you better, too."

He walked her to the door of the boarding house. "I hope you have good news about your daddy's job." He kept a smile on his face until he turned to head down the walk.

His sister crossed the line this time. He clenched his fists and stormed home almost getting hit by a car he stepped in front of. He raised his hands, "Sorry, man." The driver shook his head and drove on.

He strolled down Vine Street toward his home. His sister sat on the front porch. He walked faster. Victor leapt onto the porch and grabbed her as she opened the screen door. "Oh, no you don't. Sit, we're having a talk."

He sat Ruth Ann in a chair and leaned on the porch rail. "You crossed the line today. You and Anna going to Dottie's work and giving her a hard time. You could have gotten her fired. Don't you care about anyone but yourself?"

She ignored him.

"Look at me when I talk to you."

"You're not my father."

"That's right, I'm not. How 'bout I go in and tell him what you did?" He walked to the screen door and opened it.

Ruth Ann stood. "Victor, don't tell. I'm sorry but Anna likes you. She'd be a better girlfriend than Dottie."

He turned to his sister and shook his head. "Anna's too young. I'm not interested in her. I like Dottie and nothing you say is going to stop us from going out. I want you to tell Anna I'm not interested in being her boyfriend."

His sister glared and squinted her eyes. "I'm trying to keep you from making a big mistake."

"I'm not and if I do, it's my mistake not yours. Are you going to tell Anna or do you want me to call her parents and have them talk to her?"

"You wouldn't."

"Tell her and then keep your nose out of my business."

"I'll talk to her." Ruth Ann sat in the chair.

He glowered at his sister. "And?"

She took a deep breath. "I'm sorry."

Chapter Sixteen

Dottie entered the boarding house. The only sound came from the oscillating fan moving hot air through the bottom floor of the house. She walked to the stairs leading to her room and glanced in the parlor. Ella and Avery were sitting close together on the sofa. She walked closer and cleared her throat. They appeared to be sleeping.

A bottle of bourbon and two glasses stopped her in her tracks. "What's going on here? Are you both drunk?" She grabbed the bottle and walked through the kitchen to the back door. She stepped out on the porch and threw the bottle against the large rock Ella used to dry her house shoes on. The bottle shattered sending squirrels scattering up the pine tree. She turned, Ella stood at the door.

"He got the job, we were celebrating." Her words were slurred.

Dottie shook and her voice broke. She wanted to cry but she would not lose control. "When does he start?"

Ella searched the plank floor. "Tomorrow."

She put her hands on her hips and moved closer. "Tomorrow, and you thought getting him drunk would be a good idea?"

Ella ran her hand through her hair, a frown filled her face. "Avery wanted to celebrate. It's my fault. I'm sorry honey." She sat at the kitchen table with her head in her hands.

Dottie put coffee beans in the coffee grinder, turned the crank until the cylinder emptied and opened the drawer. She spooned the ground coffee into the percolator filled with water and sat it on the stove eye. "Can you eat scrambled eggs and toast?"

Ella stood and grabbed the table for balance. "Yes, I'll help you."

"No, sit. I'll do it." She opened the refrigerator to get the eggs and butter and turned on the stove for toast.

"We were so happy about the news. I didn't think one little ol' drink would hurt." Dottie sliced the bread cutting pieces of butter to sprinkle on top before putting the pan in the oven. "You know he can't stop at one drink." She broke eggs into a bowl and beat them with a fork. When the butter in the iron skillet melted, she poured the eggs in and stirred slowly until they were softly scrambled. "If you can walk, find Daddy and tell him supper's ready."

They ate in silence, her daddy and Ella glimpsing at her like children who'd been disciplined by a parent. "Daddy, when you're done, get cleaned up while I finish in here. I'll help you choose clothes for work tomorrow."

Avery came out of the bathroom and hugged his daughter. "I don't deserve what you do for me."

Dottie put Avery's clothes on the chair. "This suit will look nice for your first day. Get a good night's sleep and I'll wake you in the morning."

****

She heard the Cotton Mill bell ring and jumped out of bed. She ran downstairs and knocked on Avery's door. "Daddy, it's time to get up." She didn't hear anything so she peeked in. "Are you awake?"

Avery turned over and swung his feet to the floor. "Yes, thanks."

She turned to go. "I'll see you in the kitchen in a few minutes." She ran upstairs and started getting ready for work. She dressed and headed to the kitchen. Ella poured coffee in a cup. "I need to make some toast and cook a couple of eggs over easy."

Ella took a sip of coffee and sat at the table. "Sure honey, need any help?"

"I can manage."

Avery came in the kitchen.

Ella poured him a cup of coffee. "Did you sleep good, Avery?"

Avery smiled. "I did, did you?"

"Like a baby. Bourbon does that."

Dottie scowled at them and shook her head. "No more bourbon for either one of you. Here's your eggs, Daddy." She noticed the time. She grabbed a piece of toast and headed out the door. "Good luck today, Daddy. I've got to go."

Avery stood. "What's your rush? I figured we'd walk in together."

She grabbed her pocketbook and lunch bag. "I'm late, see you tonight."

She ran most of the way to Main Street. *How could time have gotten away from me so fast?*

Mr. Murphy met her at the door. "Dottie, I told you, if you started coming in late, I'd have to let you go."

She begged, "Please, Mr. Murphy, don't fire me. Daddy got a job. I had to fix his breakfast and help him get ready."

"Why do you have to help a grown man get ready for work?"

"I wouldn't usually. He got sick last night and…"

Mr. Murphy raised his hand. "Don't say anymore, I understand. Dottie, this is the very last time, if you're late again, I'm finding another clerk."

She cleaned the glass displays and unpacked boxes. She loved her job. When she worked, she didn't worry about her problems. She liked helping the customers, and although Mr. Murphy demanded excellence, she liked him. The store reflected on both of them.

Victor waited for her outside the Five and Dime. "I hope you had good news last night."

She fell into his walking pace. "Yes, Daddy got a job at Bartholomew's Auto Sales, but he and Ella celebrated. I had two drunks to deal with. I was late for work this morning. Mr. Murphy threatened to fire me. I didn't have a good day."

"I'm sorry, but at least he got a job. Mr. Murphy'll forget about you being late by next week."

"I hope you're right."

He took her arm and guided her across the street. "Are you going to the church picnic Saturday?"

"I haven't heard anything about a picnic."

"Yes, it's an annual fund raiser. The girls bring a picnic basket with enough food for two people. The baskets are auctioned off to a lucky gentleman, and the girl joins him for lunch."

"Sounds like fun, but what if no one bids on your basket."

Victor smiled. "Won't be a problem."

"I've never been to a picnic auction. What do they

do with the money?"

He took her hand. "The money goes to the Children's Home."

She smiled and walked closer. "What a good way to raise money. I'm sure lots of girls will want you to bid on their basket."

"Well, there's only one girl I'm interested in."

She silently prayed she'd be the one. "Thanks for walking me home."

"The pleasure's mine. How about going to the picture show tonight?"

"I'd love to. What's playing?"

"*One Sunday Afternoon*. I'll pick you up at seven."

She walked in the boarding house. "Ella, where are you?"

"In the kitchen. You have a good day?"

Dottie danced in the room. "I had a wonderful day. Victor's taking me to the picture show tonight."

"Sounds like fun. What are they showing this week?" Ella grabbed a towel and dried her hands.

Dottie took a glass out of the cabinet and filled it with water. "*One Sunday Afternoon*."

"That's a great movie."

She sat at the table. "He asked me to go to the church picnic Saturday. I have to take a picnic basket. The baskets are auctioned off to the highest bidder."

"What are you going to make?"

"Mama taught me how to make the best biscuits in the world. There are some blackberry bushes in the vacant lot at the end of the street. I'll pick them Friday after work." She opened cabinet doors searching for ingredients. "I need lard, milk, self-rising flour, sugar and butter. Do you have it in the house?" She turned.

"I'll pay you for what I use."

"I have everything but the butter. I'll get that from Mrs. Ward. She makes the best in the county." Ella added butter to her weekly grocery list.

"Good, I'm going to make the biscuits, and put butter, sugar and blackberries in them while they're hot. Everything melts together, and the biscuit tastes like blackberry cobbler."

Ella leaned against the sink. "Sounds good, whoever bids on your basket will be a lucky man."

Dottie hoped the person who bid on her basket would be Victor. What if he bid on Anna's basket instead of hers?

Chapter Seventeen

After the movie, Victor took Dottie to the boarding house. They sat on the front porch in the dappled light of the evening enjoying the coolness of the night. He put his arm around her shoulders, touching the skin of her arm with his fingers. The feel of her softness sent a jolt through his arm to his heart. She turned and he lost himself in her eyes. He lowered his head and kissed her. She responded, their tongues tangled and eager, he didn't want to come up for air. Never in his life had he enjoyed kissing as much. He pulled back and smiled.

Dottie turned her head. "Why are you smiling?"

He ignored her question and placed kisses along her neck until he made his way to her lips. He wanted to do more. It had been a long time since he had to hold back with a girl. She acted innocent but when he kissed her she responded with abandon making him want her more. Victor deepened his kiss. He wanted to consume her. She ran her hand over his neck. The sensation gave him goose bumps. He wanted to take her in his arms and carry her into the night. He repositioned his body on the bench and steadied his mind. He leaned into the bench, as she opened her eyes.

He straightened on the bench but kept his arm around her. "Did you like the movie?"

Dottie took a deep breath. "I liked the movie. I'm glad Biff realized he loved his wife."

"I agree. Biff confused his feelings of love for Virginia with wanting to get revenge on Hugo for marrying her. I'm glad he discovered he married the right girl."

Victor pushed her hair from her face and kissed her again. "You are so pretty and sweet. I enjoy being with you."

Dottie whispered, "Me too."

He leaned to give her another kiss. She closed her eyes and he hesitated staring at her beautiful face. He kissed her lips and she opened her mouth inviting him in. He wanted to keep her in his embrace. The simple act of holding her satisfied him, for now. He placed his knuckles under her chin, as he turned her face to his. "I've never enjoyed kissing anyone as much as you."

She closed her eyes. "I've never kissed anyone as much as I have you."

He leaned closer and whispered, "You kiss like you've had lots of experience."

She could barely whisper. "I learned from you. You can't tell me you don't have experience."

"I'm not gonna tell you anything about who I kissed in the past. I'll only say you're the best." He smiled and tilted his head.

"I'll see you later, Miss Lester." Victor stood and pulled her from her seat.

"I look forward to seeing you, Mr. Douglas."

Victor placed a kiss on her cheek, and made his way to his car.

Chapter Eighteen

Dottie sifted flour in a bowl. Using the back of her hand she created a well in the center. She scooped lard out of the can with her fingers, placing it in the middle. Using the lard left on her hands, she greased the pan and worked a little flour into the lard, keeping it in the well.

When the mixture resembled the consistency of grainy peas, she added milk and incorporated small amounts of flour to form a dough. Perfect, a puffy cloud surrounded by a ring of flour.

She could hear her mama say, "The dough is perfect, soft as a baby's bottom. Now, take a piece of dough and roll between your hands. Place the dough on the greased pan, and press with your knuckles." Tears rolled down her face. She hadn't made biscuits since Carolyn died. These were a replica of her mama's. She put the pan in the oven and noted the time. She sat in the kitchen watching the clock, she didn't want to burn them. When they were done, she sliced them open and loaded them with butter, sugar, and berries while they were hot. She made two for Avery and Ella and set them aside. She put the remaining biscuits in the basket and headed to her room to get ready.

Ella knocked on the door. "Can I come in?"

She sat at her dressing table. "Sure, come in."

Ella peeked in. "I thought you might need some

help getting ready."

"Yes, I do need your help."

She studied Dottie's face. "Let's see how you look with a little make-up."

She leaned closer to the mirror. "I have some lipstick. It belonged to Mama."

Ella moved toward the door. "Get it, and I have a trick for your lashes. I'll be right back."

She found the lipstick and a clip for her hair and laid them on the dressing table.

Ella returned with matches, Vaseline, and fresh flowers. She pulled a match out of the box. "I'm going to light the match, and let the stick burn. I'll dip the black stick in the Vaseline, and apply the Vaseline to your lashes."

Dottie sat still as the woman worked on her eyes. She gazed in the mirror, the Vaseline made her eyes look bigger and brighter.

Ella took the lipstick and blended a little on each cheek, then told her to apply the lipstick to her lips. She brushed Dottie's hair down her back. She used the hair clip to hold the top of her hair and secured the flowers to hide the clip. "You look beautiful. Do you have perfume?"

"I don't." Dottie took a mirror and turned to look at the back of her hair.

Ella ran to the door. "I'll be right back."

She studied her reflection. She couldn't believe how a little lipstick and Vaseline had transformed her face.

Ella waltzed in the room, with a little bottle. "Here you go, there's not a man alive who doesn't like the scent of vanilla. Put some behind each ear. Stand, let me look at you."

She stood and walked to the full length mirror. "I can't believe this is me. What a difference a little make-up makes."

"Yes, and the fact you're in love. It shows in your eyes. I believe Victor feels the same way."

"I've never been this excited about a fella before." She twirled on her tiptoes. "Thank you for everything you do for me and Daddy."

Ella fished something out of her pocket. "Here, I want you to wear my gold earbobs." She placed them in Dottie's hand.

Dottie stared at the jewelry. "They're beautiful. I'll take good care of them. Thank you."

Ella hugged her. "Now get your biscuits and go, you don't want to be late."

She grabbed the basket and headed to church. The anticipation of seeing Victor caused her to perspire. She walked on the shady side of the street to stay cool. She hoped the vanilla would hold out. Her mind raced. *What if he wasn't there or he bid on another basket and I'm left standing alone.* She stood in front of the church staring at the door. She opened it, letting her eyes adjust to the empty, dark space. The only light came through the stained glass windows. She wasn't familiar with the building, she'd only been there for Sunday service.

She stood still, taking in her surroundings. On the left side of the church behind the piano, a door stood partially open. She followed voices and found herself in a small hall. She walked toward the sound and opened another door. She hesitated, afraid to go inside. Baskets stood side by side on a table with some spilling on the floor.

Girls stood on the left and boys on the right. She cast about for Victor and spotted him standing with a red haired man. She nodded as he motioned for her to put her basket with the others. After placing it on the floor, she made her way to the back of the room to stand with the girls. They laughed and talked about their food.

She heard Ruth Ann say her mother had made fried chicken and potato salad. Anna's mother made ham sandwiches and apple sauce. One girl even had beef tenderloin and green beans in her basket. *What a mistake, I made biscuits, and picked berries out of the yard.* She glanced across the room catching Victor's eye. He smiled. If he bid on her basket, he would be disappointed.

Dottie recognized Clara Lowe, the preacher's wife as auctioneer. She did her best to match the couples together. Anna's basket was next, Clara smiled at Victor. She asked if there were any more bids for the basket. He ignored her and winked at Dottie. Ruth Ann's basket was next. The tall handsome red haired man started the bid, others joined in. Several boys shouted out bids, he shook his head and left. Dottie took a deep breath. Her basket would be next. Clara ignored it and selected one on the other side of the table.

One basket remained...hers. Couples laughed and strolled out of the room. She stared at the floor wishing she hadn't come. Clara placed it on the table. "We have one last basket. Do I hear any bids for this one?"

Victor raised his hand and said, "I bid five dollars for the basket." Everyone stopped talking. You could hear a pin drop in the hall.

Dottie's mouth opened and she stared. He would be

disappointed.

Victor collected the basket and his girl. "Let's go, I've got the perfect place to picnic." He guided her through the cemetery to the little pond, behind the church. He sat the basket on a cement bench near the water's edge. "Sit, let's see what we have."

She sat on the bench and watched as he opened the basket.

He took out the paper sacks and red and white checked napkins. "What do we have here?"

"Biscuits. Mama taught me how to make them."

Victor pulled the fluffy confection dripping with berry juice out of the bag and took a bite.

She held her breath afraid he wouldn't like it.

"That's the best biscuit I ever ate, but don't tell my mother. How did you get the idea to put berries inside? This tastes like a blackberry cobbler."

"Mama used to make them for us every summer. You're not disappointed?"

"No Dottie, I'm not disappointed in anything you do. You are the nicest, sweetest and smartest girl I've ever met." He reached for a second helping.

"When I started listening to the other girls talk about what they had in their baskets, I wanted to grab mine and go home."

He rubbed his hand across her cheek. "I got the best girl, and the best basket."

They finished their biscuits and washed them down with sweet tea Ella had poured into Mason Jars.

Victor placed the basket on the ground. He moved closer to Dottie and took her hand. A tingling sensation flowed through her arm, she tugged on her hand. He didn't let go.

He raised it to his mouth gazing in her eyes while he gave her hand a gentle kiss. "I've enjoyed this more than anything I've done in a long time. Tomorrow's Sunday, I'm not taking no for an answer. We're going flying. If you don't come to church, I'll hunt you down."

"I promise I'll be there."

"Good, and before we fly, we're having lunch with Uncle Walter and Aunt Delores. I keep my plane on their property, you'll love them."

"If you're sure they won't mind."

Victor put his arm around her shoulder. "I'm sure they won't mind. They'll love you."

He brushed her hair behind her shoulder and kissed her neck. He turned her head and their lips met. "Sweetest kiss I've ever had."

"Must be the sugar and berries," Dottie said as she slowly opened her eyes.

He kissed her again, and she responded timidly, at first. She took Victor's lead and kissed him the way he kissed. Long, deep kisses. His tongue entered her mouth and she reveled in the feel of it. She responded and suddenly their tongues were in an eager battle, each tugging and tasting. He sucked on her bottom lip. A sensation deep inside made her long for everything he could give. She feared her heart would beat out of her chest, but she didn't want him to stop.

He pulled away. Their eyes fixed on each other. "You are so beautiful."

She smiled and stared at the ground. "I don't know what to say."

He took her face in his hands and gave her a gentle kiss. "I better get you home."

"I had a great time with you today." She reached for the basket.

Victor took it. They walked home holding hands. When they arrived at the door, he bent like he wanted to kiss her, but Dottie turned her head. She opened the screen door and stepped inside. "Thank you for buying my basket, I had a wonderful time."

"Me too, see you tomorrow."

She walked in the kitchen to put the basket in the cupboard.

Ella sat at the kitchen table. "Did you have fun?"

She sat at the table and folded her hands under her chin. "I sure did."

"Tell me about it." Ella stood and got a pitcher of water out of the refrigerator.

"The auction started with the girls and boys on separate sides of the room. Clara acted as auctioneer. She matched couples together."

Ella rolled her eyes. "That ol' busy body. She's always sticking her nose in. I hope she didn't cause a problem with you and Victor."

"She wanted Victor to bid on Anna's basket. He ignored her."

Ella poured her a glass of water. "Good for him."

"He bid five dollars for my basket."

"A Lincoln? He must like you."

"There was a red haired man with Victor. He bid on Ruth Ann's basket. The other boys outbid him and he left."

Ella sat. "Frankie Howard. He's Victor's best friend. That's the man he bought the bi-plane from. Everyone in town knows he has eyes for Ruth Ann. She won't have a thing to do with him."

Dottie took a sip of cold water. "More boys bid on Ruth Ann's basket than any others. He didn't stand a chance unless he had a lot of money. She can be nasty. She doesn't like me much. She'd rather her brother date Anna."

"Anna's no competition for you. I've seen the way Victor looks at you. He's smitten, for sure." Ella refilled Dottie's glass and put the pitcher in the refrigerator.

"I hope you're right. I like him more than anyone I've ever dated." She heard footsteps. "Quiet, Daddy's coming."

Avery strolled in the kitchen. "Tell me about the picnic. Who's the lucky guy who got your basket?"

Dottie spoke softly. "Victor."

"I figured as much. What'd he bid?"

"Five dollars."

"That's a lot of money. I'll bet you were the prettiest girl there." Avery's eyes filled with tears.

Dottie stood and pulled a chair out. "I'm going flying with Victor tomorrow."

Avery put his hands on his hips. "Flying? In an airplane? Who's airplane?"

She took a deep breath and chose her words carefully. "Victor has a bi-plane. He flew in the United States Army Air Corp. I'm sure he's a good pilot."

Avery sat in the chair. "He'd better be. I don't want anything to happen to my baby girl."

She put her hand on her daddy's arm. "Don't worry Daddy, I'll be safe."

Chapter Nineteen

Dottie dried the breakfast dishes and placed them in the cabinet. "Can you help me with my hair and make-up this morning? I want to wear flowers again. I'm not wearing a hat."

Ella smiled. "Sure, I'll help you but there may be a scandal at church if you don't wear a hat."

"I want to give Clara something to talk about. Will you pick more of those pretty flowers?"

"Sure thing."

She closed the door to her bedroom to dress in private. She put on the blouse and buttoned the front. She stepped into the full skirt making sure the zipper was centered in the back. She opened the door and sat at her dressing table waiting.

Ella peeked in. "Ready for me?"

She studied herself in the mirror. "Yes, please."

Ella brought a basket full of the things they needed to make her beautiful.

Dottie's heart swelled with love for the sweet lady who had become her closest friend. "I want to tell you I don't mind if you and Daddy are getting close. Mama would want him to be happy."

Ella sat on the bed. "I've always had a crush on Avery. I can't believe he's showing me attention."

"You're good for him and I appreciate your help, he's been a handful."

Ella stood and brushed Dottie's hair. She pulled the top of her hair back and secured it with the hair clip. "I'm glad you came here. You're like Carolyn, pretty and sweet. I miss her."

"It helps me to talk to people who knew her."

"Carolyn would be so proud of the young woman you've become."

She dotted her eyes with a handkerchief.

Ella lit a match. "Enough talk, let's get you ready."

They entered the church at the singing of the first hymn. Dottie recognized the look of relief Victor gave her.

He stepped out of his pew, walked to the last row, and sat with her. The congregation turned, their eyes followed him. Some smiled and some didn't. Dottie's face heated from the attention.

Pastor Lowe stepped to the pulpit for the opening prayer. The congregation faced forward.

They crowded together on the bench. She could feel his thigh tight against hers. She hoped there wouldn't be a quiz after church, because she didn't hear a thing Pastor Lowe said.

Victor waited until the preacher walked to the entrance of the church then he turned to Dottie. "The good thing about sitting in the last pew, is you're the first to leave. Let's get out of here."

She turned to Ella and whispered goodbye.

She kissed her on the cheek. "Have a great time today."

Dottie pulled her into a hug. "Thanks. See you later."

He opened the car door for her, and they headed off to the farm.

Her eyes explored one side of the highway to the other. "The land is pretty out here, I've never been out this way before."

"There are lots of farms. My uncle owns a hundred acres. The land's been in mother's side of the family for two generations."

Dottie settled in. She decided to look out of the right side of the car. She would look at the other side of the road on the way home. There were miles of pasture land, and too many cows to count. Wild flowers were blooming on the side of the road. She spotted her favorite, Queen Anne's Lace. She loved the delicate white flowers on the long thin stems.

Victor parked the car. He walked to her side and helped her out. They strolled to the porch. "Uncle Walter, this is Dottie Lester."

Walter stood and extended his hand. "Afternoon, pleased to meet you Dottie."

She shook his hand. "And you too, Mr. Andrews, thank you for asking me to Sunday dinner."

Victor opened the screen door.

She entered the living room first followed by the men. She noticed two big chairs placed in front of a potbellied stove. A Zenith Stratosphere Radio sat against the wall. Next to it stood a bookcase. The titles drew her, she spotted novels, paperback mysteries, gardening journals and encyclopedias. "I've never seen this many books in one place except at a library. And the radio, it's beautiful." She walked toward the case to get a better look.

Walter followed. "Delores and I love to read, how 'bout you?"

"I do but I don't have much time now."

Delores came to the door, wiping her hands on her apron. Victor took her hand. "Aunt Delores, this is Dottie."

Delores grabbed her and gave her a hug. "Come in the kitchen with me. I need help setting the table. I hope you don't mind, we're having vegetables today. The garden's comin' in and I've been canning for a month, but these are all fresh."

She couldn't believe the bowls of food. She served corn, green beans, squash, okra, tomatoes, and sweet potatoes. "Looks delicious, did you grow all this?"

"I have a little vegetable garden behind the house where I grow herbs, and a few vegetables, but Walter grows the corn and watermelons. He has a big tractor, but I remember when he used a plow and mule. We have conveniences we didn't have when we got married. The best one is indoor plumbing. Victor must really like you he's never brought a girl out to fly before."

"Do you like to fly, Mrs. Andrews?"

She walked toward a cabinet for a plate. "Please call me Delores, and no, scares me to death. I can't understand how the airplane gets off the ground, and how it stays in the air. What's to keep it from falling? Walter loves to fly. He sneaks off every chance he gets." She pulled the iron skillet out of the stove and turned the cornbread out into the plate. "Now that Frankie, he's crazy. The last time Victor let him fly, he almost crashed into the pig pen. The plane headed straight down then all of a sudden it straightened out and climbed into the air. But don't worry, my nephew's very careful." Delores raised her voice, "Walter, Victor, dinner's ready."

She put the plate of cornbread at the head of the table. "Always keep the bread close to your man's plate. He'll appreciate you for it."

"I'll remember that." Dottie loved this sweet lady already.

"The men will sit on each end. You sit there."

She stood beside her chair waiting for the men to join them. Victor pulled her chair out and she sat giving him a big smile.

Walter prayed. "Dear Lord, thank You for this food and the good weather You gave us this year to grow it. Thank you for Dottie and Victor, please keep them safe as they fly this afternoon. We appreciate all You do for us. In Christ's name I pray. Amen."

She loved everything about the Andrews. They were nice, and made her feel welcome. She could have stayed and talked to them all afternoon.

Victor finished his peach cobbler and waited for her to take the last bite. "Time to fly."

Uncle Walter walked with them to the plane shed. "I'll get the gas can for you."

"Thanks. I'll check the engine."

She stood off to the side and watched as they readied the plane. She had an empty feeling in the pit of her stomach even though she'd eaten a big lunch. Being near the plane made her aware the only thing between her and the ground would be a man-made contraption. She didn't understand how the plane got off the ground. She had the urge to turn and run. She backed away from the bi-plane.

Victor eased toward her. "Nervous?"

"Yes, a little. No, a lot. I'm a lot nervous."

He pulled her in his arms and kissed her forehead.

"I'm not going to let anything happen to you. Once you get in the air, you're going to love it. If you don't, hold up three fingers and I'll bring you down."

Dottie frowned. "Sign language?"

Victor smiled. "It's loud in the plane. We won't be able to hear each other talk. Showing three fingers will be easy for you to remember."

She raised her hand and showed him the sign. "Three fingers it is."

He walked her to the plane and showed her where she would sit. "You sit in the front and I sit in the back."

"Why wouldn't you sit in the front, you're flying the plane?"

"The passenger or student sits in the front and the pilot in the back. There are controls at both seats but that isn't your concern. If only the pilot is flying, he sits in the rear seat in order to distribute the weight." Victor reached into the bi-plane and took out a hat and goggles. "Here put these on." He took the can and poured gas into the tank. He handed Walter the empty container and walked over to Dottie. "These caps can be hard to put on. Let's take the flowers out and it'll be easier." Victor dropped them on the ground. "I hope you didn't want to save these."

"I forgot about the daisies. No wonder I'm having a hard time."

He pulled her hair up, put the cap on her head, and fastened the buckle. He put his knuckle under her chin and raised her head. "You look better in the hat than Frankie does."

Dottie laughed. "I hope so."

Walter helped her step on the wing. "Be careful

and step next to the seat and not on the wing or your foot will go through the fabric and there won't be any flying today."

She stepped on the darkened area next to her seat. She held her skirt and climbed into the plane. She secured the goggles and tightened the strap.

Walter stepped closer and grabbed a piece of fabric. "This here is your seatbelt. Fasten it and draw it tight."

She did as she was told. "Thanks, Mr. Andrews."

Victor and his uncle pushed the plane out of the shed, to the runway.

He jumped in his seat, and said to his uncle, "Prop us off."

Dottie observed how Walter pulled the propeller, stepping away after each try. The propeller spun on the third turn. He ran to the side out of the way.

The strong air from the spinning propeller pushed her. Her ears roared from the sound of the engine. She screamed, "Wait." Her entire body shook, chill bumps shivered down her arms. She manipulated her right hand with her left trying to make the three finger sign when she heard Victor yell.

"Ready?" She had the urge to unfasten her seatbelt and jump from the plane. Alone in the front seat she yearned to see Victor.

She searched Mr. Andrew's face. He nodded his head. "Yes." She raised her voice over the roar. "Yes, I'm ready." The engine noise increased, and the air from the fast spinning propeller buffeted her.

The airplane rocked gently, picking up speed. The control stick moved slightly forward between her knees. The tail of the plane rose and leveled out. Now she could see all around. The ground and bushes rushed by faster and her heart beat quickened. Then the control stick moved rearward, the nose rose, and the wheels left the earth.

The plane rose into the air. Her stomach did a somersault. She clenched the sides of her seat, ready to jump out, but as the plane gained altitude, she relaxed and looked down. Everything seemed small from the air. As the plane rose higher, the barns and farmhouse started to disappear. She closed her eyes. Peace overwhelmed her, it was as if she were a feather floating through time. She loved flying.

The airplane headed toward town. The church steeple loomed at them. The bi-plane banked to the left, the boarding house below them. As they flew over Main Street, the plane rose to a higher altitude.

She peered from side to side observing the earth from a perspective she'd never dreamed about. The thick green forests would open to a lake or pasture then another forest would come into view. The vibration of the bi-plane swept through her body, dulling her senses. She closed her eyes and relaxed against the seat. She had no idea how long they'd been in the air.

The humming of the wires changed to a higher pitch. The airplane picked up speed. She grabbed the sides of the seat as fear clutched her heart. She closed her eyes and prayed. The bi-plane hit the pasture with a bounce before coming to a stop close to the shed.

Victor turned off the engine. He stepped out, climbed on the plane beside the seat and reached for Dottie's hand to help her out.

He jumped off the wing, grabbed her around the waist, and set her in front of him. Without saying a word, he took her face in his hands. He bent to kiss her. Her legs were weak from flying. She hadn't gotten used to being on land. When he kissed her, it was as if she were in a whirlpool, the earth spinning around her.

She swayed, Victor steadied her. "Well, how do you like it?"

She tightened her hold on his arm as the earth turned beneath her. "What, the flying?"

He pulled the aviator cap off her head. "Yes, the flying."

"I was scared at first, but when we got in the air, I relaxed and enjoyed the ride. Until we landed. I feared we were crashing." She moved her weight from one foot to the other trying to find her balance.

"I'm glad you like to fly, and I'm sorry, should have told you how the sound of the wires changes on the descent."

Walter walked toward them. "Did you have fun?"

Victor didn't take his eyes off her. "We had a great time."

She watched as they put the plane in the shed, and tied down each wheel. She leaned against a tree wondering if the weakness in her legs was from the flying, or the kiss. Victor took her hand and the three walked to the house.

Delores gave Dottie another bear hug. "Please come and visit again."

She returned the embrace. "I've had such a great day. I hope I see you again soon."

Walter scooped two watermelons. "Here's a melon for both of you."

Victor took one and Walter followed him to the car. "Thanks, Uncle Walter. You grow the best in the state."

He started the car and backed out of the driveway. "How do you feel?"

"Like I'm still flying."

"It feels good, doesn't it?"

"Yes, now I understand why you want to make a career of it."

They arrived at the boarding house as the sun set. Victor took one of the watermelons, and walked her to the door. Ella and Avery were sitting on the porch. "Good evening. My uncle sent you a watermelon."

Avery stood and took the melon. "Thank you." He turned to his daughter. "Well, how'd you like flying?"

Dottie bounced from foot to foot. "I loved it."

Avery raised his eyebrows. "You weren't scared?"

"Yes, but after we got in the air and I started looking around, I loved it."

Victor's chest swelled with pride. "She took to it like a duck in water."

Ella opened the door and Avery followed her. "Glad y'all had fun. Good to see you, Victor."

"You too, Mr. Lester."

He took both of her hands. "I enjoyed our day together. I'm glad you like to fly."

She caught her daddy staring from inside the house. "I had a wonderful day. Thank you."

He lowered his head to kiss her goodbye.

She stepped aside and whispered. "Daddy's watching us."

Victor straightened to his full height. "We need to buy you some women's trousers to wear when you fly. You'll be able to get in the plane much easier." He squeezed her hand. "See you tomorrow."

She floated in the house and found her daddy and Ella in the parlor. They asked about her day. How did she feel flying in the air high above the ground? What did everything look like from the sky? Dottie told them about their lunch, how many vegetables Delores served, and about the delicious peach cobbler. She told them everything, but she didn't tell them about the kiss. That incredible kiss would stay between her and Victor.

Chapter Twenty

Victor helped his father lock the drugstore and ambled across the street to the Five and Dime. He waited for Dottie under the awning, which provided a small amount of shade from the hot Georgia sun.

The door opened and she stepped out. "Have you been waiting long?"

He took her hand in his. "A few minutes."

"We got a lot of new inventory today and I stayed over to unpack the last box."

Victor guided her across the street so they could walk in the shade under the large oak trees. "You're a dedicated worker, I'm sure Mr. Murphy's glad he hired you."

"I hope he is, I love my job. You won't believe what happened today."

He slowed his walk. "What happened?"

"Mrs. Murphy came to the store. She acted like a customer. She criticized my thread and bobbin display. Mr. Murphy came in from the back of the store and introduced us. She became a different person, real nice and polite, like we were best friends.

He apologized after she left. Mrs. Murphy didn't want him to hire me. She wanted the position. She helped him open the store fifteen years ago.

They had different ideas about how the store should be run. She had their first baby and wanted to stay home. Now that the kids were older, she wanted to work. I've had a few weeks of excitement, with Mrs. Murphy, Mrs. Douglas, Lisbeth, Ruth Ann and Anna. I can't wait to see what happens next week."

Victor laughed. "Sometimes I wish we had excitement. The only people who come in the drug store are either sick or hungry."

"Do you like working with your father?"

"He's very smart. I learn something new from him every day. But, working in the drug store is not what I want to do for the rest of my life. How's Mr. Lester?"

"He hasn't touched a drop of whiskey since he started his new job."

"He's lucky to have a daughter like you."

"We've had our share of arguments over his drinking. I'm not going to take it like Mama did."

"Well, you don't have to. He has to accept responsibility for his actions."

"Yes, he's beginning to understand."

They arrived at the boarding house, Victor took both of her hands. "Would you like to come to supper tomorrow night? Ma wants to spend time with you, she's jealous because Aunt Delores cooked for you first."

"Thank you, I'd love to."

"Well, Miss Lester, I'll see you tomorrow."

He found his mother in the kitchen. "Dottie's coming for supper tomorrow night."

"It's about time you brought her for a visit. Don't worry about Ruth Ann, she'll behave, I'll make sure."

"Thanks, Ma."

Hattie removed the lid from a pot of beans, steam rose as she stirred them. "What's her favorite food?"

He sat at the table. "Not sure, but she can make some good biscuits."

"I'll make cornbread. I don't want to show her up in the biscuit department."

He stifled his laugh, if it came to a contest, Dottie'd win hands down. After supper he drove out to visit Frankie. He wanted to check on him. They hadn't talked since the picnic and he lost the bid for Ruth Ann's basket. Frankie sat on his front porch talking to a neighbor. Victor parked in the side yard and walked to the porch. The man said hello, then headed to his house.

"Well, stranger, I thought you had forgotten about me. I spotted the Jenny flying Sunday, did you go by yourself or did Mr. Andrews sneak off with you?"

Victor sat in the empty chair. "I wasn't alone, I took Dottie up."

"Ah, that pretty girl. Did you get her basket?"

"I did, we had a nice lunch and a good day flying Sunday."

"I guess she took my place at Mrs. Andrews' Sunday dinner table."

"She did, Aunt Delores had more leftovers than she does when you eat with us."

"Sounds like things are heating. You like her?"

"I like her. She's not like anyone I've ever been involved with."

"What makes her different?"

Victor studied the blue sky dotted with clouds. "Have you ever been with someone who makes you a better man when you're with them? That's how she makes me feel."

"What're you gonna do?"

"Not sure. I've invited her over for supper

tomorrow night with the family."

Frankie tilted his head. "Better put a sock in Ruthie's mouth."

"Yeah, about her. I'm sorry about what happened at the auction Saturday."

"Oh, I knew I'd be outbid. Those spoiled boys she hangs out with are high class. Their parents make sure they have enough money to buy what they want. Have you heard from Delta Air Lines?"

"Nothing yet. Uncle Walter and I had a talk last week, he offered me forty acres to use to build an airport. He said he would leave me all the land when he and Aunt Delores are gone."

Frankie's eyes lit up. "Oh man, can you imagine? Your own airport. Planes flying in and out all the time. You'd have to build a small tower and sheds for planes. You'd need some employees and I know someone who has experience." Frankie hesitated waiting for Victor to look his way. "We could give flying lessons and do crop dusting. What'd you tell him?"

"I told him I appreciated his generous offer, but I applied for a job. I had to wait until I heard from them before I gave my final answer."

Frankie stood and walked to the edge of the porch. "Victor, you've got more than anyone, a pretty girl friend, a family who loves you, an uncle going to give you land to start a business, and you can't wait to leave everything behind."

He stood and walked to the edge of the porch, turning his back to Frankie. He didn't face him until the sun set on the field. "You have some good points but I planned my career from the first time I spotted a plane in the air. If I get a job offer, I'm taking it."

Frankie put his hand on Victor's arm. "I'm not one to give advice. You've made better choices than I have. I should've planned a career. I wouldn't be working in the Cotton Mill."

He started down the front step and turned. "We'll fly Saturday if the weather's good."

Frankie leaned against the two by four holding the porch. "I look forward to it."

He started his car and swerved to avoid the ruts in the dirt and gravel road. His car had been stuck in the holes too many times. He didn't want to pay for another clutch, or replace a tire. He wished he could help Frankie get out of the mill, and make enough money to move to town. They would be good partners in an airport, or any business. He loved Frankie like a brother, but if he got the job, he would take it. No matter who or what.

Chapter Twenty-One

Dottie changed her dress three times. "Do you like this one?"

Ella tilted her head, crossed her arms, and studied her. "I like all of them. Which one feels more comfortable?"

"What's comfort got to do with it?"

"A lot, if you're my age. I'm sorry honey, I don't blame you for being nervous, but they're people like us."

She pulled the dress over her head and reached for another one. "What if they don't like me?"

"You've met them all except Mr. Douglas. Ruth Ann's a handful but you shouldn't have a problem with Hattie or Lisbeth."

"How is Mr. Douglas? Is he nice?"

"Mr. Douglas is a nice man. Very serious, but kind."

"I heard a knock, must be Victor. I'll be out in a couple of minutes."

Ella opened the door. "Hi Victor, have a seat, Dottie'll be ready soon."

He sat on the sofa holding a box. "Thank you."

Dottie strolled into the parlor. He stood and handed her the present. "This is for you."

"Victor, you didn't have to buy me anything."

He nodded toward the package. "Open it."

She opened the lid and pulled out a pair of tan women's trousers. "They're beautiful, thank you, I love them. Does this mean I get to ride in the Jenny again?"

"You can ride in the Jenny anytime you want, how 'bout Sunday?"

"Sunday's a date, Mr. Douglas."

"Oh, and you can bring them and change at the farm, no need to wear them to church."

"They would kick me out of church if I wore them," Dottie said, flashing a smile to light a dark room.

She ran upstairs and placed the box on her bed. She glanced out the window. Victor's car sat at the curb. Thank goodness, they weren't walking to his house. Her feet still hurt from working. The only shoes that matched her dress belonged to Carolyn and were a half size too small.

They settled in the car. Dottie stared out the side window.

He watched her tug her knuckles. "What's wrong? You look nervous."

"Can you tell? I am a little nervous about supper with your family."

"Don't be, I promise they'll be on their best behavior. Ruth Ann knows better than to start anything."

"I've never formally met Mr. Douglas."

"He can be a little gruff but it's the way he is. Don't let him intimidate you."

"Now, you've got me worried."

"When he gets to know you, he'll discover what a great girl you are."

Hattie met them at the door. "I've got a few more

things to do, you two come in. Dottie, make yourself at home."

Lisbeth bounced into the room. "Hi Dottie, want to hear my new song. I'm learning to play 'Puttin' On The Ritz.'" Lisbeth pulled her toward the piano. "Do you sing?"

Dottie answered a timid, "A little."

"Have you heard 'Puttin' On The Ritz' before?"

"Yes, I've seen the movie too."

Lisbeth sat on the piano stool while she stood. Lisbeth started with the introduction but stumbled over a few notes. "I don't have the song perfect yet, the introduction is a little difficult but I can play the rest pretty good. My teacher says the rhythmic pattern in this song is the most complex she's seen in a popular song."

She played the introduction again and they started singing. Dottie came in too soon on the Puttin' On The Ritz words. They doubled over with laughter.

Lisbeth took a deep breath and stopped playing. "Let me play the piano section leading into that part."

She listened and hummed the words. "I've got it."

Victor stood in the door watching and joined in singing a few lines. Hattie danced into the living room and he grabbed her hand and spun her.

Jacob walked into the room. "Henrietta, is supper ready?"

Everything got quiet. Hattie's laughter broke the silence. "Yes, supper's ready. I came in here to gather everyone."

Victor reached for Dottie's hand. "Pa, I'd like for you to meet Dottie Lester."

"Pleased to meet you, Miss Lester."

"The pleasure is mine, Mr. Douglas."

Victor rolled his eyes. "Such formality, let's eat." He guided her to the kitchen. "You sit here." He pulled her chair out, she adjusted her skirt and sat.

Hattie said a short prayer then handed Dottie a platter. "I'm glad you could join us for supper tonight. I hope you like beef roast."

"Yes ma'am, I do." She put some roast on her plate. Victor passed her a bowl of potatoes. She took the bowl and placed a spoon full of the fluffy creamed potatoes next to her roast. "Everything looks delicious. We usually have a sandwich or bacon, eggs and toast for supper."

Hattie nodded. "It takes time to prepare a meal like this."

Dottie placed some sliced tomatoes on her plate. "Yes, Ella and I cook a nice meal on Sunday for the boarders. I enjoy helping her."

Hattie announced, "I made a sweet potato cobbler for dessert."

Jacob smiled at his wife. "Thanks, Henrietta, it's my favorite." Jacob nodded at his daughters. "What did you girls do today?"

"We went swimming at the park," Ruth Ann answered while reaching for her glass of ice tea.

Lisbeth took a roll from the bread basket. "I hate to see summer come to an end. We'll have to go to school."

Ruth Ann gave Lisbeth a smug smile. "A couple more years and I'll go to college."

Hattie's lips turned down. "My kids are growing too fast."

Victor glanced toward his sister. "I'm proud you

want to pursue an education. Most of the girls in my class only wanted to get married and have kids."

Jacob stared at his daughter. "Yes, I'm proud of you, too."

She grinned from ear to ear. "Thank you."

Hattie and Lisbeth cleared the dishes, while Ruth Ann put the cobbler in bowls.

Dottie took a bite of the dessert. The sweet potatoes were soft. She could taste the cinnamon and butter. The flaky crust crumbled as she scooped the cobbler on her spoon. "This is wonderful. I've never had a sweet potato cobbler before."

Hattie shook her head. "Really? We have it all the time."

She licked her lips. "Is it hard to make?"

Hattie placed her spoon in her bowl and gave the young woman her full attention. "The trick is to peel and slice the sweet potatoes and boil them in water with a little bit of sugar until they are almost fork tender. Then you put them in a casserole dish with butter, sugar, cinnamon, and a little water. I use my biscuit recipe for the topping. Victor said you make good biscuits."

"Mama taught me how to make them. She cooked like you. This meal reminds me of ones she prepared for us." Everyone finished their dessert, and Hattie removed the bowls.

Dottie stood. "May I assist with the dishes?"

Hattie took the spoons and bowls to the sink. "No, the girls will help. Y'all go with Jacob into the parlor. We'll be there shortly."

Jacob questioned her about where she went to school and if she graduated. "It's a shame, most boys and girls have to quit school and work to help their family. Most of my customers have worked at the Cotton Mill since they were twelve or thirteen years old."

She agreed. "I'm very fortunate Mr. Murphy hired me."

Jacob nodded his head. "Yes you are, I'm sure you're a good worker. Mr. Murphy doesn't hire anyone but the best. Our family is one of the lucky ones in town who can send their children to college."

"I wanted to go but Mama got sick and I had to take care of her."

"You're young, you can still. I'm proud Victor went into the service but I'd rather he got a degree. I wanted him to take over the pharmacy."

Dottie listened to Mr. Douglas talk about his son. The man she loved would not be happy dispensing medicine. She observed Victor, lost in thought. How long would he be here? Everyone wanted him to stay in Saplingville, especially her.

Hattie and the girls joined them. Ruth Ann suggested a game of charades. Everyone participated except Jacob. He watched and laughed as the others did their silly motions. She didn't want the night to end.

Victor walked her home. She pulled her shoes off. They walked with their arms around each other's waist. Clouds darted across the moon, the only light coming from a few street lights. When they reached the darkest point, Victor stopped and pulled her into his arms. They kissed until she had trouble getting her breath, he backed away.

Victor smoothed her hair. "Sorry, I didn't mean to smother you."

"I'd give up a little air for a kiss from you anytime."

He pulled her close until their bodies melted into each other and gave her a deep kiss. His arousal pressed against her, the nerve endings in her entire body on high alert.

Victor focused. "You don't know what you do to me."

Dottie smiled. "I have a general idea." She put her finger on Victor's lips. "And you, you make me so weak I can barely walk after you kiss me."

"I don't mind carrying you the rest of the way home." He kissed her and lifted her into his arms. He carried her a few steps before he put her down. They neared the boarding house and he removed his arm from around her and took her hand. "I had a great time tonight."

"I did, too. Now I see what it's like to have a big family."

"We have good times and bad like everyone else." He opened the screen door. "I'll see you tomorrow."

Dottie opened the front door and stepped inside. "Thanks, Victor."

She walked into the quiet house. Ella left a lamp on in the parlor which gave a soft glow helping her make her way upstairs. She entered her room and closed the door. Enough moonlight came in for her to see the chair in front of the window. She sat and relived the events of the night. She hugged her knees to her chest and closed her eyes.

Remembering his kisses, she forgot to breathe. She opened her eyes and gulped for air. She glanced at the clock counting the hours until she could see him again.

Chapter Twenty-Two

Victor walked the few blocks home. He didn't want to leave Dottie. She belonged with him, it would be like losing an arm when he left town. He loved his family, but saying good-bye to them would be easier than leaving her behind. He could ask her to go with him, but would it be fair? He wouldn't be in one place very long, and probably wouldn't have his own house, only a room to keep his things and a place to sleep on his few days off.

He meandered through the yard. Ruth Ann sat on the front porch. "You're up late tonight."

"I couldn't sleep."

"What's on your mind?"

"I'm sorry about how I treated Dottie. She's a nice girl."

Victor studied his sister. "What's got into you?"

"I'm thinkin' about how I've been acting lately, and some of the things you've been telling me. I haven't been nice to Dottie or Frankie. I'm jealous of Dottie. She's on her own, has a job and takes care of herself. She has an independence I envy. Frankie, well Frankie gets under my skin because he knows me."

He sat on the top step. "Yes, you and Frankie are alike in lots of ways. You're both fearless and reckless, but you're also smart and caring."

She settled beside him. "I talked to Pa about

school. He wants me to go to Judson in Marion, Alabama. Judson is an all girl's Baptist College."

He stared at his pretty sister's profile. "He figures you won't get in as much trouble there."

She stood. "I'm going to try to stay out of trouble. I have to prove I can take care of myself. I want to go to Alabama College in Montevallo, Alabama. I read about their Little Theater in the *Theatre Arts Monthly*. Will you talk to him?"

He nodded. "I'll see what I can do."

They went in the house, and Victor locked the front door. "Night, Ruth Ann."

His sister went in the living room, grabbed the latest *Redbook* magazine, and sprawled on the sofa. "Night, Victor."

Chapter Twenty-Three

Victor waited in the heat for Dottie to come out of the Five and Dime. "How'd you like my family?"

She came out of the door and put her arm through her pocketbook handle. "I love them, especially Lisbeth. I had fun singing our duet. Mrs. Douglas is a great cook. Do you eat like that every night?"

He took her elbow and guided her across the street. "Yes, we do most nights. We had a little extra last night because of you. We don't usually eat out of the good china during the week."

Dottie stepped on the sidewalk and pulled her elbow out of his grasp. "They made me feel important."

He reached for her hand. "You were our honored guest. How'd you like my father?"

"Is he always so business like?" She wrapped her fingers around Victor's hand.

"Yes, I'm afraid he is."

"I don't mean it in a negative way." Dottie studied his profile.

"That's how he is. He reads and studies a lot, so he's kind of introverted." Victor's eyes met hers. "I knew what you meant."

"Well, he's a very nice man. I enjoyed spending time with your family."

"They enjoyed you too."

They arrived at the boarding house. He kissed her

on the cheek and walked the few blocks to his house. His mother waited at the door, a look of anticipation on her face. "You got a letter today," Hattie said holding a blue envelope with white banding.

"Thanks, Ma."

He climbed the stairs to his room and closed the door. He put the letter on his desk and walked to the window. He glanced at the letter, afraid to open it, but more afraid not to. The letter would change his life whether he got a job interview or not. Decisions had to be made, if he got an interview he'd get the job of this he was certain. He sat at his desk, opened the letter, and let out a sigh of relief. He had an interview in two weeks. He ran down the stairs and kissed his ma on the cheek.

"I'm going to see Uncle Walter. I'll be back later tonight. Don't worry about my supper."

****

Victor spotted his uncle working on his tractor and walked over to the barn. "I need to talk to you about something."

Walter wiped his hands on a rag and they walked to the porch. They settled in their rockers. "What's on your mind?"

"I got a reply from Delta Air Lines. I have an interview in two weeks. I'm going to fly to Atlanta. My old car won't make it."

"Ought to make a good impression, you flying your own plane. I'm real proud of you. Have you told Jacob?"

"Not yet. I'll wait until a few days before I go. I don't want to upset him." Walter's hound dog grunted as he settled at his feet.

"He's a strong man. He'll be proud of you, in whatever course you decide to take."

"I hope so, this has been my dream since you took me to see the barnstormers. The way they flew their planes first so straight and then diving and twirling in the air. The spins, dives, loop-the-loops and barrel rolls were amazing. When the wing walkers climbed out of their seats and stood on the wings, I closed my eyes. You made me open them and watch. Their tricks appeared easy. It took a lot of nerve to stand on the wings. The pilots had the responsibility of keeping the planes steady and straight, not knowing when a gust of wind would come."

"Yes, and now you're going to fly commercial airliners."

"I can't believe it." Victor scratched the old dog behind the ear.

"You've worked hard for this day. Look at the awards you won in the service for flying." Walter stopped rocking.

"I did my duty." Victor deflected the compliment.

Walter stood and leaned on the bannister. "Maybe so, but you excelled and now you can reap the rewards. The deal still stands, if this doesn't work out, you always have a place here."

"I appreciate that." Victor stood and shook his uncle's hand. "See you later, Uncle Walter."

He turned his car toward home, but decided to drive by the boarding house. Dottie and Avery walked down the sidewalk. Avery weaved back and forth as Dottie struggled to hold him. He stopped the car and jumped out.

He grabbed Avery. "Get in the car, Dottie."

She shook her head. "No, I can take him home. You don't need to get involved in this."

He shoved the drunkard in the front. "Dottie, get in the back."

She shuffled to the other side and climbed in.

Victor got in the driver's seat. His jaw ached from gritting his teeth. He slammed his door, the latch didn't catch. He slammed it again. Under his breath he said, "Son of a bitch." He took a deep breath, relaxed, and pulled up until it caught in the latch.

She leaned over the front seat. "Daddy didn't come home so I went looking for him in town."

Victor glowered at Avery slumped in the front seat. "I'm glad I noticed you. You aren't strong enough to support his weight." He stopped in front of the boarding house. She ran to help her daddy out of the car. "No Dottie, let me get him out. You go ahead and open the front door."

She ran to the porch and waited for Victor to drag her father up the walk. "His room is there to the right."

He led Avery to the kitchen. "He's not going to bed. Get me the percolator and coffee, please."

She filled the pot with water and ground beans for the percolator basket. "I'll fix it for you."

"No, leave us alone. I want to talk to Mr. Lester." Dottie stood in the door.

"This is man's business," Victor said as he pushed her and closed the door. He put the coffee pot on the stove and found two coffee cups in the cabinet. He considered the drunk, his head resting on the table. He shook him. "No, old man, you aren't going to sleep this one off."

"Who are you to tell me what to do?" Avery

slurred his words.

Victor jerked him from his chair and pushed him against the wall. "I'm the one who is going to stop you from treating Dottie like the baby sitter of a drunk. You don't deserve a daughter like her."

He let go of him and Avery stumbled to his chair. He poured a cup of black coffee. The man took a couple of sips and ran to the door. He ran after him but he didn't have to worry about him running off. He turned his head and closed his ears to the sound of a drunkard hurling his guts out.

Avery staggered and grabbed the tree trunk for support. Victor led him in the house and poured more coffee. "You aren't much of a man Mr. Lester."

Avery set his cup down. "You may be right, but I do love my baby girl."

"Your baby girl is a woman now, she works to support you, gives you food and a place to live. She worries about you. She nurses you when you're so drunk, you don't know where you are. You don't love her or respect her. You may have loved the baby girl you had, but this woman is giving her life for a drunk. This stops tonight, here and now. You have a choice, you can stay in this town, work and support yourself, or you can leave and let Dottie live her life without the likes of you."

Victor watched Avery's shoulders shake. He poured more coffee and made dry toast. They both sat in silence for a long time drinking coffee and eating.

Avery spoke, "I've been a fool, but my life's hard. I drink to forget about my problems. It's easier."

"Easier for you in the moment but harder for those who love you. You're making everything worse for all concerned. I can't imagine how much it hurt to lose your wife but she's gone. You need to move on with your life and let Dottie move on with hers. You're not being fair. Your daughter is proof she had good parents who raised her right. You can become the man you were, your choice to make."

Avery nodded and drank more coffee. "I don't care about anyone when I drink, only my sorry self. I'll do better."

They stood, Victor stuck out his hand. Avery stared at it, then reached and shook. "You need to talk to Pastor Lowe and ask for prayers to help you overcome this."

Avery agreed, "Yes, it's time."

Victor opened the door to the kitchen.

Dottie hugged her father. "Daddy, are you okay?"

Avery kissed the top of her head. "Yes, don't worry, I'll be fine."

Victor put the cups in the sink, and rinsed out the coffee pot.

She kissed him on the cheek. "Thank you." Avery stumbled to his room. Victor pulled her into his arms. "Mr. Lester shouldn't have any trouble going to work in the morning."

Dottie walked him to the front door. "Thanks again."

He placed a gentle kiss on her cheek and walked to his car. He'd been drunk and he'd seen Frankie drunk many times. They loved to party and have fun and could take it or leave it. Mr. Lester was a drunk, plain and simple. Victor would never understand how a man could put his family through the hell and humiliation. Dottie needed protection and a future.

Chapter Twenty-Four

Dottie welcomed customers as they came in the Five and Dime. It gave her a respite from worry over the events of last night. Any thoughts she might have of them spending their lives together disappeared into the night along with her dignity. No one would want to be a part of a family like hers. Should she apologize or act like nothing happened? She dreaded quitting time, afraid Victor would be outside the door but more afraid he wouldn't.

He stood under the awning. She hesitated and took a deep breath before opening the door. "Victor, I'm sorry you had to see Daddy drunk last night."

He placed his hands on her shoulders. "Dottie, I'm glad I could help you. Don't worry about anything."

"I'm embarrassed." She stared at the sidewalk.

"I understand but you shouldn't be. His drinking's not your fault."

"I used to imagine if I could be smarter, or prettier, or a better daughter."

He turned her face so he could gaze into her eyes. "That's ridiculous."

"Now that I'm older, I understand him better."

"Dottie, don't worry. I'll help you whenever you need it." He guided her across the street.

"Thanks, Victor."

His hand found hers. "I also told Avery he needed

to talk to Pastor Lowe. Your daddy needs prayers. He needs to put his trust in the Lord, not the bottle."

"I agree, only God can help him overcome his addiction."

They walked down the shaded side of the street. She dreaded the answer but had to ask. "Did you hear anything about the job interview?"

"As a matter of fact, I did. I have an interview in a couple of weeks."

She ran ahead of him and turned grabbing his hands. "Victor, that's great, I'm happy for you." Dottie hid her disappointment with a smile.

He gazed into her eyes. "Thank you. It's what I've worked for my whole life."

She walked closer. "When will you start?"

"I'm not sure, they're forming a new company. I sound like I have the job and haven't been to an interview. I'd better not count my chickens before they hatch."

"What'd your parents say?"

"I haven't told them. So far the only one I've talked to about this is Uncle Walter."

"What did he say?"

"Uncle Walter's happy for me, he's the reason I fly. He took me to see my first flying circus. A group of men were flying bi-planes like the one I have."

"How old were you?"

"Twelve. Since then, not a day has gone by I haven't dreamed about flying."

They continued to walk, the silence thickened by the minute. "I'll miss you."

He squeezed her hand. "I'll miss you too."

They paused on the walk in front of the boarding

house. He didn't meet her eyes.

He kissed her on the cheek. "I'll see you tomorrow."

She sat on the swing and watched him. Every step he took away from her snatched pieces of her heart. When he was gone, there would be nothing left.

****

Saturday morning, Dottie stood by the window and watched her daddy polish the 1934 Chevrolet Master Sedan. Mr. Bartholomew allowed him to drive new cars home for advertisement. She marveled at how he'd changed since Victor confronted him about his drinking earlier in the week. He met with Pastor Lowe for counseling and planned to start going to church. Dottie and Ella doubled their watch of him never letting him out of their sight. She got the feeling Ella enjoyed taking care of Avery. She fixed her hair and make-up and made sure he had plenty of good food. Seeing a woman other than Carolyn give her daddy attention broke her heart but her mama would want him to find someone and be happy.

They prepared a picnic lunch of fried chicken and biscuits. Dottie wrapped the catheads in a towel while Ella poured cold sweet tea into jars.

Ella organized the food in the basket placing a large towel on top. "I'll get a couple of quilts from the closet and meet you at the car."

Dottie lifted the towel and took in the smell of the chicken before grabbing the hamper. She couldn't wait to get outside to enjoy the morning.

Avery met her at the bottom porch step. "Let me take the food."

She stepped on the side board and climbed in the

backseat. "Wow, there's lots of room in here."

He placed the basket beside her. "It's a nice car." He put the quilts in the floor and opened the passenger door for Ella. Before closing the door, he peered inside. "There's no place on earth I'd rather be than with you two. Thanks for putting up with this old man."

A happy tear slid down her cheek. She sat in a new shiny car. People stared and waved as they rode on the highway out of town. She was spending the day with the ones she loved.

As they neared the lake, she watched for the gravel road. "Turn right."

Avery pulled the car over on the grass. "This is a good spot."

She jumped out of the car and twirled gazing at the sky. The rain from the night before cooled the morning and the shade from the oak kept the sun from beating down on them. "Give me a quilt."

She spread the quilt on the ground. "Victor said they would fly over sometime after noon."

The three sat on the quilt. Avery leaned against the tree trunk, closed his eyes, and started snoring.

Ella pulled her from the quilt. "Let's walk around the lake. When he wakes, we'll eat lunch."

Chapter Twenty-Five

When Victor and Frankie arrived at the farm, Delores met them at the door with country ham biscuits and hot cups of coffee. They all sat on the front porch visiting and eating.

Frankie finished his off first. Delores offered him another. "You're a jewel Mrs. Andrews, thank you."

"I've told you to call me Delores and I love taking care of my boys. You need strength to fly, and I want you to come back safe, you hear."

Victor watched Frankie enjoy the attention. "I'll let you fly today Frankie."

"You will?"

"Yep, but I want a nice day in the sky. Dottie, Ella, and Avery are having a picnic at the lake and I told her we would fly over. You can do a loop for them. They should still be there about the time we return from flying to the Alabama line. Dottie and I are flying tomorrow."

Delores gathered the dishes. "If y'all fly tomorrow, I'll fix lunch for you. I like her."

"Thanks, Aunt Delores. I bought her some women's trousers to wear so she'll need to change clothes here."

"How thoughtful of you. I don't know how she crawled in that hole of a seat with a dress on."

They hugged Delores and walked to the field with

Walter. Victor admired how the three of them fell into their duties to get the plane ready. After Frankie untied the wheels, Walter pulled the chocks from each wheel while he checked the engine. Frankie and Walter added gas to the tank and walked around the plane inspecting the wings and cabling.

With the pre-flight check complete, they pushed the plane out to the make shift runway, making sure they would take off into the wind. Frankie climbed in the rear and Victor in the front. Uncle Walter propped them off and Frankie started taxiing.

The engine dominated the front of the plane. The large bi-plane wing structure made visibility difficult. Frankie S-turned so he could see if everything was clear for takeoff.

The bi-plane lifted into the wind and rose to five thousand feet. He appreciated Frankie's skills. The wing walkers wanted to fly with him, because he could keep the plane steady and straight as an arrow, while they did their stunts.

He enjoyed the peace the skies gave and would have gone to sleep, but he didn't want to miss a minute of his time in the air. Frankie flew the Jenny like a seasoned professional.

The two hours passed quickly. On their descent Victor could see the lake and spotted his friends. The plane banked to the right as they flew over. The three jumped to their feet gazing at the plane. He saluted and Frankie waved. The plane ascended to get in the position for the loop. After the loop, Frankie took the plane into a figure eight maneuver before heading to the field where he made a perfect three point landing.

Victor jumped out of the plane and patted Frankie

on the back. "You did some great flying today."

"Thanks, means a lot coming from you."

He dropped Frankie off at his house and headed to town. He missed Dottie and couldn't wait until tomorrow. She sat on the front porch reading an Agatha Christie book. Victor took the porch steps two at a time. "How was the picnic?"

She set the book on the side table. "We had a wonderful day, especially when you and Frankie flew over. When the plane looped, I thought you were going to crash. Daddy liked the figure eight. The stunts are amazing from the ground."

"I told Frankie he could do a loop but don't worry, I won't be doing any when you're in the plane. I'm glad Avery got to see the Jenny. I don't want him to worry about you flying. It's better if he has an idea of what the plane looks like."

He moved closer and grabbed her hand. He loved how their fingers fit together so easily. He raised it to his lips and kissed it. She leaned over and kissed him on the cheek.

"Thanks for coming by tonight. This is a pleasant surprise."

"I wanted to tell you, Aunt Delores insists we eat lunch with them. She said you could change there so don't forget your trousers."

Avery and Ella made their way outside. Dottie tugged on her hand but he wouldn't let go. He gave her a big smile. Her hand relaxed in his.

Her daddy and Ella sat on the porch swing. Avery got the swing going in a slow rhythm. "We enjoyed seeing your airplane today. How fast does it fly?"

"The top speed in the Jenny is seventy-five miles

an hour."

Dottie turned. "Seventy-five miles an hour? When we're flying, it feels like we're floating in the air."

He smiled and turned his gaze to Avery. "If you like, I'll take you for an airplane ride." Dottie squeezed his hand.

Avery straightened in his seat. "Yes, I'd like it very much. When?"

"How about tomorrow after we go up. Around three o'clock?"

"Sounds great. I'll be there."

"Drive to my uncle's farm and park at their house. I'll tell them you're coming. Uncle Walter will show you where we keep the plane."

Chapter Twenty-Six

After a delicious lunch with the Andrews, Dottie excused herself to change into her trousers. She walked into the dining room.

Victor let out a wolf whistle.

Delores pulled her into a bear hug. "You look so pretty, how do they feel?"

"I love them. I wish I could wear them all the time. I feel like Katherine Hepburn."

He couldn't take his eyes off her. "You're prettier than Katherine Hepburn."

She stared at the floor. "You always know what to say."

She followed Victor and Walter to the plane shed. Victor handed her the aviator cap and goggles. She struggled with the cap, but this time she had it on before they finished the safety check.

Victor smiled when he discovered she was ready to fly. "Come, I'll help you in the plane and we'll push it to the runway."

She stepped in the right spot. The women's trousers made it easier to navigate the small area and get in her seat. She raised her goggles to the top of her head so she could see the inside of the plane. She took time to study the gages and the stick which moved so smoothly when they were flying. She didn't dare touch anything.

Victor climbed in his seat. "Ready to go?"

She turned nodding her head. "I'm ready." She placed the goggles over her eyes and fastened her seatbelt. Walter turned the propeller.

When the engine fired and the propeller started spinning she wasn't afraid of the wind, she embraced it. She kept her hands in her lap and didn't grip the sides like she did on her first ride. She couldn't wait to get in the air. She had more nerve this time, and didn't take her eyes off the ground, until the plane straightened and headed for the Alabama line. The vibration of the airplane and the whirl of the singing cables created a tranquil atmosphere.

Her love of flying, and her love for Victor intensified as the bi-plane ascended. She rode high above the earth with him at the controls of her life and her heart. A disappointment crept over her when she spotted the runway and recognized the now familiar descent of the bi-plane. Avery and Walter stood under the oak tree waiting.

Avery ran to the plane and helped her out. "How was it?"

"Great. You're gonna love it."

Victor and Walter did another check of the engine, oil, and gas.

Avery clinched his fists, stared at the plane and then the sky. "I'm a little nervous about this."

Victor walked over and put his hand on Avery's shoulder. "Relax and enjoy the ride, Mr. Lester."

Avery took a deep breath. "I never thought I would fly in an airplane. I was eleven years old when the Wright brothers made their first flight."

Victor nodded. "Flying has certainly changed since

then."

He handed Avery the hat and goggles.

Dottie helped him put them on and fastened the strap. "Relax and have fun."

Avery pulled at the hat. "I'll do my best."

Dottie walked to the shed. Avery settled in his seat and she prayed they would be safe. She watched the plane rise from the ground and stared at the sky until the Jenny flew out of sight.

Dottie and Walter watched for the plane to return. When they spotted it, they walked to the shed and waited.

Avery couldn't contain his excitement. He climbed out of his seat and jumped to the ground. "Amazing. Thank you."

Victor shook his hand. "I'll take you up anytime. I'm glad you enjoyed it."

Avery put his hand on Victor's shoulder. "I accept your invitation."

The four people worked together to secure the Jenny in the shed. Dottie and Victor said goodbye to Avery and headed to Frankie's house.

The car slowed as he turned down a dirt road. He guided the car around giant holes. She held onto the dash as the car swayed back and forth. The shanty town came into view. People were sitting on porches or under large oak trees. Kids were playing and dogs chased after them. All of the houses needed a coat of paint. Dottie and her daddy were poor but they lived better than these people. They may not have much, but folks in the shanty town were friendly. Everyone waved and the kids chased the car until they parked in Frankie's yard.

Frankie ran out to greet them. "Hey, thanks for coming by."

Victor opened her car door. "I wanted you to meet Dottie."

She stepped out of the car and put her hand out for the tall man to shake.

He ignored her hand and gave her a hug. "Dottie, I'm glad to finally meet you. Victor says lots of good things about you."

She stood on her tiptoes as Frankie hugged her and lifted her off the ground. He put her down and she regained her footing. "It's nice to meet you. I've heard so many great things about you. We loved seeing your aerobatics yesterday."

Victor cleared his throat. "We stopped by on our way home from Uncle Walter's house."

Frankie let her walk ahead. "I lost count of how many times the Jenny flew over today."

She sat in the chair Frankie placed on the little porch. "After Victor took me up, he took my daddy for a ride. He loved it."

Frankie smiled at Dottie. "How about you? Do you like flying?"

"I do but the first time, I didn't relax until about fifteen minutes into the flight."

Victor teased her. "Really? Any other secrets you want to share?"

She laughed. "None I'd tell you."

Frankie stepped into the house and pulled two more chairs out to the porch.

Victor placed his chair next to Dottie. "I want to stay until dark. This is the best view in town for the sunset."

She watched the giant yellow ball settle into the horizon and listened to Frankie tell barnstormer stories. He could spin a yarn but she had a feeling the dare devil told the truth. He didn't appear to be afraid of anyone or anything. On the way home she asked Victor, "If Frankie is such a great pilot, why can't he get a job flying?"

"Frankie's only trained in flying the Jenny. The JN-4 is an out of date plane. There are many new ships with different engines and flight instruments. Frankie isn't trained for today's planes. I was lucky to get in the USAAC where I trained on the newest and best. I need to get a pilot job soon before I'm in the same boat. The airlines won't hire you without experience flying passenger ships."

She laughed, "I get confused when you say ships and planes. Why do you call them ships?"

"The terminology is a pilot thing, especially if we're talking about new planes." Victor slowed the car as they neared town.

"How could Frankie get experience?"

"He needs more training and flight time. It would take money he doesn't have."

"It's a shame someone as talented as he is can't get a break."

Victor parked the car in front of the boarding house. He hurried to open her door. "I've been wanting to do this all day."

He pulled her close and gave her a long, deep kiss. She ran her fingers through his hair then pulled away. Someone watched them.

They made their way to the porch, her daddy sat in the dark smiling. "Hey you two, I wanted to thank you again for taking me flying today."

Victor shook his hand. "We'll fly again." He walked to his car, turned, and waved.

Dottie sat next to her daddy and put her head on his shoulder.

He put his arm around her. "Victor's a good man. I'm glad you met him."

Tears streamed down her face. "I'm glad I met him, but he's leaving town soon. I'll never see him again."

Avery took his arm from her shoulders and turned her face toward him. "Where's he going?"

"He's a pilot, Daddy, flying will always be the most important thing in his life. The little Jenny isn't enough. He wants to fly commercial airliners. He and Frankie are the smartest and most unusual men I've ever met. They have a silent passion, it consumes them and controls their path in life. Men like them are destined to fly. The sky wants them as much as they want the sky. I couldn't stand in his way any more than we can bring Mama back to us." She wiped tears from her face. "When he leaves, I'm moving to Macon with Aunt Bess. I want to find something I can be passionate about. Meeting him taught me we're all born for a reason. I want to find my reason, Daddy."

Avery cupped her face with his hands. "Oh, baby girl, you are so special. You proved it, when you took such good care of your mama. You cared for me when I was too stupid to help myself. Your life is only beginning. You can do anything you set your mind to. I'll support you, and help you any way I can to make your dreams happen."

They made their way into the house to get ready

for work the next day. She carefully folded her trousers and laid them on a chair. She would wear them to work tomorrow.

Chapter Twenty-Seven

Victor spent most of his workday staring out the front window toward Murphy's Five and Dime. Knowing Dottie worked just across the street helped him make it through his day. After locking the store and doing his cleaning chores he walked into the sunshine. He stood under the awning when she came out the door. "Wow, you must like those trousers to wear them to work."

She shuffled her feet. "Mr. Murphy fussed about them this morning. I cleaned the lower shelves and the floor under the shelves. He forgot about the pants and commented on what a good job I did. I love the freedom to move and bend over."

"I'm sorry I missed seeing you bend over and stuff."

She pulled back to hit him and he dodged her fist. "Oh, you."

He grabbed her hand. "How 'bout going with me to the Wednesday Night Supper at the church? Everyone brings a dish. You can bring those good catheads you make. Tell Mr. Lester and Miss Simons, they may want to come too."

"Are you sure you're not looking for an excuse to get more of my biscuits?"

"You know me like a book, but they're not all I'd like to get more of."

"You're going to make me blush."

Victor bent brushing a kiss across her lips. He studied her face. "Yep that's what I like to see, you're really pretty when you blush."

She grinned. "So, what goes on at these suppers?"

"The men assemble the tables and chairs so the women can put their food out. Everyone fixes their plate and we eat for about an hour. After supper we go in the church for a singing. Sometimes we have a visiting quartet or a family group performs." They crossed the street.

"Sounds like fun. I want to go and I'm sure Daddy and Ella will."

"How does Mr. Lester like his job?"

"He likes it. I don't know what you told him but he's a changed man." Dottie missed the step to the sidewalk and grabbed his arm.

He steadied her. "Careful. I'm glad he's doing better. The job will keep his mind off his problems and maybe from hitting the bottle again."

She paused. "I love Daddy when he's sober, but I can't stand him when he drinks. He turns into another person. Ella's good for him and their friendship has helped. I feel like I've known her my whole life. We are boarders, but she feels like family."

"Miss Simons and your mother were friends. I'm sure she's happy to spend time with you."

"I'm not sure what I would have done without her."

Victor couldn't be near Dottie without touching her. He pulled her in an alley and pressed her back against the wall of the building.

Her eyes widened, but instead of pushing him

away, she pulled his head so she could reach his lips. He responded with a kiss almost crushing her into the wall. Her body molded against his like they were made for each other.

He kissed her until the heat within both of their bodies rose to the simmer point. He had to stop, but he didn't want to. Miss Dottie Lester made him weak with hunger for her, and only her. He treaded further into dangerous territory exploring her curves and her soft breasts. He liked a little bit of danger. That's what he loved about flying. Coming to his senses, he backed away and planted a gentle kiss on her lips. He took her face in his hands. "I guess we'd better stop before I can't."

Dottie closed her eyes and took a deep breath, "Yes," was all she could say.

Chapter Twenty-Eight

When Dottie arrived home her face flushed red and her nerve endings stood on alert. She helped Ella put supper on the table. Her hands shook spilling milk on the counter.

Ella said, "What's wrong?"

"I'm fine, a little nervous. It's Victor, when I'm with him, I get so weak. Sometimes I feel like I'm going to faint."

"Sounds like you've got a case of love sickness." Ella placed the plates on the table.

"Have you ever cared that much about anyone?"

"I have, once." She walked to the silver wear drawer and handed Dottie the forks.

"What happened?" She took the forks and placed them next to each plate.

"He didn't feel the same way. He moved away and I haven't seen him since. When you love someone, the feelings don't go away because they do."

"How do you deal with these feelings?"

"You go on with your life. If you're lucky someone else comes along to help you forget."

She studied her face. She could see Ella had been beautiful at one time. Who did Ella love as much as she did Victor? She could close her eyes and smell his after shave. Her lips still burned from the stubble of his beard. This, she would remember the rest of her life.

Chapter Twenty-Nine

Victor moved toward home rehearsing the words he would tell his father. It was time to tell them about his interview. The last thing he wanted was to disappoint his parents. They told him they were proud of his accomplishments in the USAAC. With luck they'd take this news good. After supper he followed Jacob to the living room.

He observed his father read the evening paper. "I need to talk to you about something." He shifted to the edge of his chair.

Jacob lowered the paper. "I'm listening."

"Delta Air Corporation has resumed its mail service out of Atlanta. They're starting a passenger service and changing their name to Delta Air Lines. I've applied for a position as a pilot for their passenger service. I have an interview next week."

Jacob folded the paper and laid it on the side table. "Is this what you really want to do?"

"This is what I have to do."

Jacob searched his face. "I wish we weren't so different."

"We aren't, you had a dream and became a pharmacist. You've worked hard to make your dream come true. You've given us more than we deserve. I'll always appreciate what you did. But, my time is now."

"I agree but I worry about you. I wish I understood

more about flying and airplanes. I grew up riding a horse everywhere I went. The idea of flying never entered our minds."

"Pa, air travel is changing fast. If I don't get in now, I never will. What about you, will you manage without me?"

"The first time an airplane flew over this town, the twinkle in your eye told me what your future would be. I've been trying to accept your decision to fly for a long time. Yes, we'll be fine. Henrietta can help until I find someone."

Victor started to get up but remembered his sister. "One more thing, I talked to Ruth Ann. She said you wanted her to go to Judson."

"Yes, it's the best school. She needs supervision and an all girl's Baptist facility fits the bill."

"I agree she's been a handful lately, but I've also seen another side of her in the last month. She wants to go to Alabama College."

"Not possible, she isn't mature enough to be on her own."

"Pa don't close your mind, give her a chance to prove she's ready, then decide."

"I'll take your suggestion into consideration." Jacob opened the newspaper and started to read.

"Thanks, Pa, for everything." He stood to leave.

"You're welcome." Jacob lowered the paper. "Son, what are you going to do about Dottie when you leave? She's a sweet girl and I hate to see her hurt."

Victor stood in the doorway. "I'm not sure. It won't be fair to her either way. If I marry her, she'll be by herself most of the time, and if I let her go, well that's something I have to live with."

"Good luck son, you can drive my car to Atlanta."

"Thanks, I'm planning to fly if the weather's good, but if not, I'll take your car."

Jacob's words about Dottie hit home, hard. Flying would always be his first concern. It was selfish but he wouldn't give her up until he had to. He loved the thrill of being with her, seeing her laugh and kissing her sweet lips.

Victor walked to the boarding house after supper. He and Dottie sat on the porch with Avery and Ella.

He reached for her hand moving his thumb along her soft skin. "How's the job, Mr. Lester? Are you selling many new cars?"

"We did a trade in last week. There are only a few people in town who can buy new cars. Most of our business is used car sales, so we were happy to get a trade in."

"Pa bought a new car the year I returned from the service and gave me his old one to drive. My car drives fine, but I wouldn't take it on a long trip."

"I can fix you up in a new one." Avery scooted to the edge of his seat.

"Not my priority right now, but thanks."

"I hear you're going to a job interview soon." Avery nodded to his daughter. "Dottie told us about it."

"Yes, I'm ready to get back in the air, flying on the weekends isn't enough. Airplanes are changing as fast as cars. The commercial planes fly twice as fast as my Jenny." The tension in the air was as thick as fog.

"Good luck, I hope you get the job." Avery glared. "If that's what you want."

Dottie set her attention on her father. "Daddy, Victor invited us three to the Church Supper on

Wednesday. I'm making biscuits."

"Well, if you are making your special bread, I'm going." He turned to Ella. "How about you?"

She smiled. "I'd love to go."

He relaxed when Avery and Ella went in the house. The sun had set leaving the porch covered in darkness. He could hold her close and kiss her without anyone seeing them. He loved how she melted into his arms. He kissed her lightly at first and when she responded, he wanted to consume her right there on the porch. Did Avery know he ravished his daughter with kisses? He almost laughed when he remembered the glances between her father and Miss Simons.

They were probably doing the same thing at the very same moment. He drew away from Dottie. He respected her and as much as he wanted to go further, he couldn't. How he wished he would be her husband. He wanted to touch her in places no man had ever explored and watch her disappear into rapture. He brought them out of their trance. "I've got to head home, if I don't we'll go to sleep on this bench. What would the neighbors say in the morning?"

"I guess you're right."

He stood, pulled her close, and kissed her goodbye.

Chapter Thirty

Victor and Dottie arrived at the Church Supper as Clara ordered the men to set up the tables. He started to help, but decided to stand aside and watch the fiasco. First, the men arranged the tables the way Clara wanted and then she changed her mind.

Pastor Lowe stepped in and told them to put the tables the usual way. Clara said she wanted to place them in a more efficient way. Pastor Lowe told her the new way wasn't efficient, if the men took an hour to organize. She then went to harass the ladies. She wanted the salads on a separate table from the vegetables. She got her way leaving no room for desserts. The sweets were placed at the end of the meat table. Victor smiled and prepared a table for drinks.

He and his family went through the food line. He noticed everyone putting dessert on top of their food. He did the same thing because he feared the chocolate cake would be gone if he waited.

He noticed everyone's plate. Cake or pie topped off their meal. "I guess we were all afraid there wouldn't be any sweets left since Clara placed the desserts at the meat table."

Avery nodded. "I've never had dessert first, I kind of like it."

Everyone laughed and their table became louder than any other family table.

Jacob noticed they were the only ones left in the room. "My, my, we've got to get in the church or we'll miss the singing."

The service featured a family group from the next county. The husband, wife and a son and daughter sat on the first row. Lisbeth sat at the piano, and Victor led the congregation in a G. T. Speer song, 'The Dearest Friend I Ever Had.'

He sat with his girl and Lisbeth moved from the piano to the front row. Pastor Lowe introduced the singing family. The group sang some toe tapping gospel along with traditional hymns. By the time they finished, the congregation stood clapping and cheering.

Pastor Lowe stepped to the podium. "I'd like Victor to close our service. We've had a request for him to sing 'In the Garden.'"

He stood and sashayed to the front of the church. He smiled and acknowledged people as he walked. He stepped to the podium and nodded to Lisbeth. She started the introduction and he came in on just the right spot. He finished the song to applause thanking everyone as he walked to his seat.

Dottie whispered. "I didn't know you could sing."

Victor gave her a sideways grin. "There are lots of things you don't know about me." He placed his hand over hers.

****

Victor walked Dottie to the boarding house. "Did you enjoy the Church Supper?"

"Yes, I hated for the night to end. They saved the best for last when they asked you to sing."

"We always had music in the house. The entire family would gather around the piano and sing while

Ma played."

"So, that's where Lisbeth gets her talent."

"Yes, Ma doesn't play as much as she used to. She served as the church pianist until Lisbeth took over. Ruth Ann's talent leans toward the theater. She loves to dance, sing, and act."

"Well, she does have an imagination. The play she and Anna put on in the store should be on Broadway."

His voice softened. "I had a great time tonight. I love when you're with me and my family."

"I love being with you and your family. Thanks for including Daddy and Ella."

She placed her head on his chest. He put his hand on her head running his fingers through her silky hair. He got lost in the softness of it. He kissed the top of her head and pulled her face to meet his. He kissed her lips and planted another kiss on the top of her head. "I had a great time, I hate to leave you."

Dottie pulled him closer and kissed his mouth.

She kissed him like a woman now, instead of a shy girl, and he liked it. He didn't want her to stop, but he had to get away. "Dottie, I had a great time, I'll see you tomorrow."

She opened her eyes. He pulled her close, her body molding against his. Guilt nagged at his belly. He should do it now. Tell her she wasn't part of his plans. "Dottie?"

She snuggled closer against his chest. "Yes."

He gritted his teeth. The longing in his groin ensnared him. He checked to make sure no one could see them. He backed in to the oak tree pulling her close. His hand brushed against her breast. Her nipple hard under her thin dress. He encircled it with his thumb.

She took a deep breath. "Victor, I…"

He wouldn't let her say it. He kissed her like a man headed to the electric chair. She moved her hand to his hard shaft. He groaned craving more, wanting everything. He teetered on the edge. The cross over easy, coming back impossible. He buried his face in her hair memorizing the scent. "Gotta go."

She gave him the sweetest smile he'd ever seen. Her face flushed, a red ring from his rough kisses framed her lips. "I know."

He walked toward the street turned and gave her a wave. The walk home gave him time to cool down. How long would it take after he left to get over his need of her? Days, months, years?

Chapter Thirty-One

Victor woke to a cool morning. The breeze coming through the window kept him snuggled under the sheets. The realization of what day it was bolted him from the bed. He ran to the window, beautiful blue skies. A perfect day to fly to Atlanta. He dressed in his best suit. He tied the laces of his freshly polished shoes and drifted downstairs to the smell of bacon and coffee.

When he arrived at the farm, Uncle Walter and Aunt Delores sat on their porch waiting.

They walked to the shed. Uncle Walter helped ready the Jenny for takeoff. He shook his hand. "Good luck."

Delores gave him a hug. "Be careful."

He settled in his seat and yelled, "contact."

Walter nodded. "Contact." He spun the propeller until the engine fired.

Victor saluted and taxied down the make-shift runway. He leveled the plane off at five thousand feet, and settled in for the forty-five minute flight to Candler Field.

All the way to Atlanta, he rehearsed what he would say to the interviewer. The questions would be the same he would ask of a pilot he would employ.

As he neared the airport and searched for a place to land, he sensed the excitement he experienced when he flew bombers in the USAAC. He missed the hustle and bustle of landing at a busy airport, and he loved the camaraderie with other pilots. He hoped he would have a good landing. He could land the JN-4 easier on a grassy field. He bounced a little but got her under control. One of the ground crew guided him to a tie down spot.

He jumped from the plane. "Hi, I'm Victor Douglas. Where would I go to apply for the Delta Air Lines Pilot position?"

"John Stewart. Nice to meet you. Go to the Eastern Air Transport Building, second floor, south corner."

"Thanks, Mr. Stewart."

He ambled to the terminal taking in the smell of open air mixed with oil and gas fumes. He spotted a Stinson T Tri-Motor airplane. Passengers were boarding and the pilot and co-pilot stood to the side.

He introduced himself. "Hi, I'm Victor Douglas. Just admiring your ship."

"I'm William Sand and this is my co-pilot Edmond Hamby. We watched you come in. Not bad for landing a Jenny on concrete."

Victor laughed. "I normally land in my uncle's field."

Edmond Hamby asked, "Were you a barnstormer?"

"No, I bought the plane from a friend who was one of the best in Georgia. I flew in the USAAC. I'm applying for a job with Delta today."

William Sand smiled. "Good luck to you, we need pilots like you."

Victor shook their hands. "Thank you."

The terminal bustled with passengers arriving and departing, and porters carrying luggage and carts with bags of mail. He took a deep breath and headed up the stairs. He stood behind a long line of men. Peering to the front, he spotted a desk with the sign 'Applications for Delta Pilots Here.' He reached the head of the line and took a clipboard with an application.

He quickly filled in his personal information but took more time with his flight information. They wanted detailed notes about the planes he flew and flight time. The more experience a pilot had, the better chance of getting a job. He handed in his application and waited with the others. Most of the men were quiet and polite, but there were a couple of boisterous braggarts.

They probably hadn't done the things they talked about and wouldn't make the cut. Pilots were a rare breed of men. They were courageous and self-assured. A good aviator was born not made. Cockiness could get you killed. He had a friend in the service who didn't have the confidence to fly. The man hid his insecurity with his better than everyone attitude. He got in trouble flying over the Pacific. The pilot, unable to bail went down with the plane.

He heard his name called and headed to the office of Mr. M. Posey.

The man stood and extended his hand. "I'm Mr. Posey."

Victor gave him a firm handshake. "Victor Douglas."

Mr. Posey sat and took his application. "Please, take a seat."

Victor sat in the chair opposite his desk. He gazed around the room while Mr. Posey studied his papers. A large map of the United States hung in a frame. From the floor to ceiling window he could see the runway where a Boeing-Stearman Model 75 Biplane landed. There were two people in the plane, one probably a student. Had to be, a trained pilot would never land with so much bounce.

Mr. Posey finished reading his application. "You were in the USAAC."

"Yes, stationed at Rockwell Field, California, for four years."

He put the application down and gave Victor his full attention. "What did you fly?"

"I took flying lessons before I went in the service. I flew whatever bi-plane I could get my hands on. In the service, I learned to fly in a P-1 Hawk, a Curtiss Model 34. I then flew the Keystone LB-6 and Keystone B-3A Bombers."

The interviewer gazed over the top of his glasses. He had to assure the man he would be cool under pressure, especially when the lives of a crew and passengers were at stake.

Mr. Posey shook his head. "Bombers? Must have been nerve wracking."

"Yes sir, flying bombers would be, if you aren't trained. They taught me to take every precaution and do everything by the book in order to avoid any disaster."

Mr. Posey nodded. "Yes, the USAAC has trained some good men. We hire a lot of you guys. I see you've been out eighteen months now. What are you doing with your time?"

"I have a JN-4 Jenny I fly when the weather permits."

"Glad to see you have a plane, but aviation is changing daily. We're flying Stinson T Tri-Motors and will be getting some Douglas DC-2's before the end of the year. Do you have the skills to adapt to these planes?"

Victor straightened in his seat. "Yes sir, as you see on my application, I have extensive training, and I'm willing to learn."

Mr. Posey took his glasses off and placed them on his desk. He picked up a piece of paper and handed it to Victor. "Mr. Douglas, I like you, you might be what we're looking for. The next step is a flight physical. Take this paper and go to the first floor, Room 103. A doctor and nurse will be waiting. We'll review your application and physical results and get back to you in two weeks. The flight training starts in September. Good luck to you."

He took the paper and shook Mr. Posey's hand, "Pleasure to meet you sir. Thank you."

He hurried down the stairs for his flight physical. There weren't as many men waiting. The two men who were loud and talkative in the interview waiting room weren't there. The nurse called Victor into the room and performed all of the tests. No doubt, he would pass. He'd been through the same examination in the service. She left the room and the doctor came in and did his physical check-up.

Dr. Blane studied the nurse's notes. "Your physical exam is good, I don't see any problems. The eye and hearing results are both normal. It will take about a week for your blood work."

"Thank you, Dr. Blane. I look forward to hearing from you."

Victor couldn't feel his feet touch the ground as he walked to the Jenny. He rehashed everything in his brain on the way home. He went over the conversation with Mr. Posey. He wished he had asked how many pilots they were hiring. Delta may only hire five and there would be others who had more flight time. He would only dwell on the positive. He had to get this job. He wanted to fly more than anything in the world. He landed and turned off the engine. He jumped out and helped his uncle guide the plane to the shed.

Walter tied down the wheels. "Glad to see you arrive safely, how'd the interview go?"

"Pretty well. I got to the flight physical stage. They said they would notify me in two weeks."

"Many people applying?"

"Yes, quite a few. I enjoyed being at the airport with the planes and pilots, I've missed the excitement."

"I'm sure you'll get the job." Walter placed the chocks under each wheel.

"You're prejudiced, Uncle Walter." He threw a piece of canvas over the opening of the bi-plane seats.

His uncle grabbed the other side, together they pulled and secured the ties. "Maybe so, but I know a good pilot when I see one."

"You should let Frankie teach you to fly the Jenny." He gave the bi-plane an inspection then walked toward his uncle.

"I thought about learning to fly. Decided I'd go for a ride with y'all when I can. Where you headed now?"

He grinned. "I'm heading to town to see a pretty girl."

He wanted to kick his heels and run to the car. The excitement of the day played through his mind like a movie. The ride to town quick, he parked on the street and smoothed his hair with a comb before stepping out of the car. He glanced at the porch anxious to see his girl. He spotted her reading a book on the bench.

She ran down the walk. "How'd your interview go?"

He took her hand as they walked to the porch. "My interview went very well. They gave me a flight physical. Mr. Posey said I would receive a letter in a couple of weeks."

"What's the airport in Atlanta like? Were there lots of planes?"

"Yes, Candler Field's quite large. When I landed, I passed by a plane loading for take-off. I met the pilots, nice men."

"How many people would the plane hold?"

"Ten people and the crew. Mr. Posey, the man who interviewed me said they would get larger planes called Douglas DC-2's by the end of the year. Those planes hold fourteen plus crew."

"Victor that's so exciting, I'm happy for you." Dottie spoke softer. "I'll miss you."

He placed his arm around her shoulder. "I'll miss you too." He kissed the top of her head. "I'll come home every chance I get."

"I'm sure your family will enjoy seeing you."

"What about you? Can I see you then?"

She hesitated before she answered. "I'm moving to Macon with my aunt."

He explored her pretty brown eyes. "I understand. Dottie, as much as I would love to take you with me, it wouldn't be fair to you. A commercial pilot spends half of his time in the air, the other half waiting to go up. I can't offer you a life like that, you deserve more."

She bit her lip. "Victor, I've enjoyed every minute with you. We've had fun and I'll always remember my first airplane ride."

The earth moved out from under him. When he recovered he said, "Let's wait and see what happens, I may not get the job."

"I don't doubt for a minute you'll get the job. You always get what you go after Mr. Douglas."

He kissed her longer than he should in the light of day and headed home.

****

Victor arrived at home in time for supper with the family. He told everyone about his interview. The table abuzz, they wanted to know all about it. After supper, he and his father went into the living room.

Jacob patted his son on the back before he sat in his favorite chair. "What kind of plane will you fly?"

"Right now they're flying Stinson T Tri-Motors."

"I've read about the new Douglas DC-2 and the Boeing 247."

Victor's eyes grew large. "You've heard about those new ships?"

"Yes, I've been reading about them. I may not be a fan of flying like Walter, but I find aviation interesting."

He couldn't hide his excitement. "Yes sir, aviation is in constant change."

Jacob softened his voice. "I am proud of what you have accomplished and what you will do in the future."

"Pa, that means so much. I always believed you were disappointed in me."

"Never disappointed, worried because I didn't understand why you were so fascinated with flying. I started studying about it when you joined the service. Aviation reminds me of medicine, there's always something new on the horizon."

"That's what excites me. The airplane builders improve on every new ship they build. You can't imagine the feeling of climbing into the cockpit of a new plane and seeing what new gages they added, or seeing how much faster the new ships can fly."

"When will you know if you get the job?" Jacob walked to the radio and turned it on.

"They said they would notify me in two weeks." Victor stood.

His father adjusted the volume and settled in his chair. "Good luck son, I hope you get it, if that's what you want."

"Thanks, Pa."

He took the stairs two at a time. He undressed to his underwear and climbed in bed. He laid awake half the night reliving the excitement from his interview and being at the airport in Atlanta. Then there was Dottie. He had to accept the fact if he got this job, he would never see her again.

Unable to stay in bed another minute, he paced the floor of his bedroom. One scenario after another played in his brain. One vision disturbed him more than anything. He got the job, came home to visit and found Dottie happily married.

He climbed between the sheets. He had to get some rest. The adrenaline coursing through his veins reminded him of the night before he flew his first bomber. He turned on his side and closed his eyes until sleep overtook him.

He dreamed he was flying a bomber and a storm came. He struggled unable to control the airplane. The clouds turned into people. The two loud mouths from the interview were there along with Uncle Walter, Dottie and Frankie. The plane started heading for earth and he bailed out.

He woke as his parachute opened. He jumped out of his bed and inspected his surroundings. Water beaded on his forehead. He grabbed a t-shirt and wiped his face. He walked to the window estimating the time to be between twilight and dawn. He dressed and made his way downstairs.

Chapter Thirty-Two

Victor stood outside the Five and Dime. A summer thunderstorm had just passed through and steam rose from the sidewalk. The humidity caused his shirt to stick to his back making him uncomfortable and edgy.

Dottie exited the store. "Hi. Some storm, huh?"

He hesitated and let her walk ahead. "Yeah, haven't heard thunder that loud in a while." They crossed the street. "Did you have a good day?"

"Pretty good, you?"

He reached for her hand, then pulled back. "Fine. Busy as usual." He attempted conversation, but she only responded with a yes or no answer. The tension between them as heavy as the humidity in the air.

They arrived at the boarding house. He stopped before walking her to her door. "I need to go now. I'm going to ride out to see Frankie tonight."

"Tell him hello."

He put his fingers under her chin. He raised her face so he could gaze into her brown eyes. "Let's go to the picture show tomorrow night." He stopped before he told her it would be their last date.

She took a deep breath. "That would be nice. See you tomorrow."

After supper, he drove to Frankie's house with leftovers.

He turned on the dirt road, avoiding the potholes

filled with water from the storm. Frankie sat on his porch with his feet on the rail. He pulled in the yard, got out of his car, waved to Frankie and walked to the passenger side for the brown paper bag.

Frankie walked to the car to meet him. "Hey man, long time no see. Whatcha got there?"

"Ma sent you leftovers from supper." He walked with his friend to the porch. Frankie opened the screen door and let him enter the house first.

He took a plate out of the cupboard. "Thanks, I haven't had a good meal since Sunday dinner with your aunt and uncle. What's going on?"

He opened the bag and placed a chicken leg on Frankie's plate. "I had my interview yesterday."

Frankie took a bite of chicken. "How'd the interview go? When do you start? Boy this is good."

He smiled at his friend enjoying something he took for granted, a home cooked meal. "The interview went fine, Mr. Posey said he would send out notifications in a couple of weeks."

"What'd Mr. Douglas say?"

"Well, he surprised me. He said he's happy for me. He's been studying aviation. He knows as much about the new ships as I do."

"No kidding?" Frankie reached in a drawer for a spoon to tackle the potato salad. "Did you see anything new at the airport?"

"Nothing I haven't seen, but Mr. Posey told me Delta ordered DC-2's. They'd have them by the end of the year."

"Oh, man, I'd love to fly those. These are the best biscuits."

"No, my friend, Dottie makes the best biscuits."

"What you gonna to do about her?"

Victor walked to the screen door. "She's going to be hard to leave."

"You'll find someone. She's not the prettiest girl I've seen you with, and you left them easy enough."

He chose his words carefully and turned to face his best friend. "She isn't the most beautiful, but she's the best girl I've ever had. Leaving Dottie's going to be tough."

Frankie stared. "We all make choices, sometimes good and sometimes bad. What makes a man is how he accepts his choices and moves on."

"Wow, Frankie, I didn't know you were so philosophical."

"I've got a lot of time to think out here, alone in this shanty town. Like Mr. Douglas, I've been reading too. I don't want to stay where I am for the rest of my life." Frankie pulled the paper off the last bowl. "Banana Pudding. I hit the jackpot tonight."

A heaviness filled his chest. He wouldn't have his best friend to confide in. His life would never be the same. "You've been the best friend a man could have. I'll miss seeing you."

"You too, but I understand you have to do this."

"I'm leaving the Jenny with you. Uncle Walter won't mind you coming and going at the farm, you're family."

Frankie put the bowl of banana pudding on the table. "I can't take the Jenny. You could sell her and make some money."

"She was yours first. Be careful and don't try any of your aerobatics. Aunt Delores' heart can't take it."

Frankie laughed. "I might even get her to go up

someday."

"Good luck with that."

"Thanks, Victor. I might start my crop dusting business. I could work for the farmers on the weekends and work at the mill during the week, save my money and leave the mill behind."

"Now you're talking." He gathered the bowls. "Let's fly on Saturday, if the weather permits."

"I look forward to it. Tell Mrs. Douglas thanks. I really enjoyed my supper. Tell your pretty sister hello."

Victor walked to the door. "I'll see you Saturday."

Chapter Thirty-Three

Dottie sat in the rocking chair with her eyes closed. She tried to wrap her thoughts around the happenings of the last few weeks. Victor had changed into another person. She wanted to reach out and pull the old Victor into her arms, make things like they were when they met.

Ella knocked on the door. "Can I come in?"

"Sure, come in."

She sat on the bed. "You seem sad, and you're barely eating anything. What's wrong?"

"Victor had his interview yesterday. I'm sure he's going to get the job and leave. I'm trying to get used to the idea of never seeing him again."

"I'm sorry honey. I thought he might change his mind. He's crazy about you." She pushed Dottie's hair away from her face.

"He's more crazy about his career. This is what he's been working for his entire life. I can't stop him. I'm not sorry we met. I wouldn't have missed it. The memories will stay with me the rest of my life." She fumbled with her handkerchief.

"I understand. I have memories I'll never let go of myself." Ella stood.

"I'm glad you and Daddy are getting to be more than friends." Dottie stood and met the woman's gaze.

"I'm sorry if you believe us getting together is too

soon after Carolyn died."

"No, Daddy needs someone. You're the best thing that's happened to him in a long time. I appreciate your help in keeping him straight. He hasn't been drunk in a while, and he seems to be doing good at his job."

"He said he would take me to church Sunday." Ella turned toward the window. "People will talk about us."

"Don't worry. People are going to talk one way or the other. I may wear my pants to church on Sunday. That would be more of a scandal."

Ella laughed. "You're gorgeous in those women's trousers. The ladies may talk about you but give them a few weeks and you'll see other women wearing them."

"Well, Mr. Murphy didn't like it, until he noticed how much work I could do in them."

"Honey, try not to worry. God has a plan for your life. If Victor isn't the one, another man will come along. Everything will work out for the good of those who love the Lord."

"Thanks, Ella. Mama told me the same thing, but God took her away from us, and I can't understand why." Dottie sat.

"We don't know why God put some people on this earth to live their full lives and takes others when they're young. That's His plan, and we have to accept it. Trust in Him, He won't leave you or forsake you."

Dottie sobbed, her entire body shook.

Ella knelt beside her chair and took her in her arms. She patted her back, "Go ahead and cry, you're strong and you'll get through all of this."

She dried her eyes with her handkerchief. "I'm going to live with Aunt Bess when he leaves. She said I shouldn't have a problem getting work in Macon. I need to go. Daddy has you and his job."

Ella brushed her hair from her face. "I'll miss you but I understand, everything here will remind you of Victor. There you can get a fresh start."

"I hope Daddy understands."

"Your leaving will be hard, but he'll understand."

Chapter Thirty-Four

Victor waited by the front door for his father. He glanced at his watch. They were five minutes late leaving for work. He turned at the sound of his father's heavy footsteps on the stairs. Jacob clung to the bannister until he reached the bottom step where he collapsed with a loud thud on the wood floor.

In two strides, Victor knelt on the floor cradling Jacob's head and shoulders. "Pa, are you all right? Pa, can you hear me?"

Hattie ran in the room from the kitchen. She froze and put her hands over her chest. "Is he?"

He put two fingers on Jacob's wrist detecting a slight pulse. "He's alive. Get me a wet rag."

His father opened his eyes. "What happened?"

"You passed out. Are you in any pain?"

Jacob used his son as a crutch and stood. "My chest hurts. You need to get me to the hospital."

Hattie hurried with a wet towel. "Forget about that. Get me Pa's car keys. We're taking him to the hospital."

His mother surprised him with her calm response. She grabbed the keys and helped him get Jacob to the car, without saying a word. The ride to the hospital only took a few minutes.

He parked the car. "I'll be right back with a wheel chair." A nurse ran out with him, as he told her what happened.

"Mr. Douglas, I'm Marge, we're going to help you in the chair." She pushed the chair while Victor helped his mother.

When they entered the hospital, someone called. "Take him to room nine. I'll find the doctor."

He stood with his mother watching Marge and the orderly settle him in the bed. Dr. Herschel called them out in the hall where Victor explained what had transpired. "We'll take it from here. As soon as I'm done, I'll find you." Another nurse took them to a room where she offered them coffee.

Hattie took Victor's hand. "We need to pray for Jacob."

They closed their eyes and both silently prayed he would be okay.

Hattie dried her eyes with a handkerchief. "I knew he didn't feel well. Lately he's been tired when he came home from work. He started taking a nap before supper. He's never done that before. He always came in and read his medical magazines. I couldn't bear to lose him."

He consoled his mother. "Don't jump to conclusions; he's going to be fine."

He'd noticed his father's declining health. He usually stood at the counter all day filling bottles and talking to customers, but lately he had been sitting on a stool, and his face pale as the vanilla milkshakes Victor made day after day. He also noted his father had stopped arguing about his plans. They waited two hours before the doctor came to see them.

Dr. Herschel walked in the room. "Mr. Douglas had a heart attack. We're doing everything we can. The situation will be touch and go for a few days."

Hattie let out a sob. "Can I see him?"

"Yes, you can. He needs to stay calm and quiet, but he will probably do better if you're here. I don't want anyone but family in his room and only two at a time."

He and Dr. Herschel walked out in the hall. Victor shook his hand. "Thank you, doctor. Is he going to get over the heart attack?"

"I'm hopeful. If he does, he's going to have to rest for a couple of months. I don't want him to go to work too soon and have another one. I advised him at his last check-up to slow down."

"He never told us. We knew he had a heart problem, but he never complained."

"Well this time you know, so you can make him rest. I'll keep you posted everyday on his progress."

"Thanks, Dr. Herschel. We appreciate everything you're doing."

He walked with his mother to the hospital room. Jacob lay in the bed asleep. Hattie sat in a chair while he stood at the window. They waited for any movement from Jacob. He finally opened his eyes and Hattie took his hand.

Jacob straightened, using his elbows for support. "I love you, Henrietta. Don't worry; I'll be fine."

Hattie smiled and cried at the same time. "I love you too. You'd better get well soon. I don't like you not being home with me."

He admired how his parents loved each other, and weren't afraid to show their affection.

Jacob regarded his son. "What about the drug store?"

Victor walked toward the bed. "Pa, I'm not

opening the store today, I'm going to make sure Ma has something to eat and is taken care of. First, I'm going home to see about Ruth Ann and Lisbeth. They were asleep when we left and must be worried. I can open the store tomorrow if you want."

"That's good, thanks for taking care of us. I love you son."

"I love you too, Pa. I'm going home but I'll be back soon."

He drove home to tell his sisters. When he arrived, the girls were outside. They'd been to the neighbors searching for their mother. When the ladies spotted the car turn in the driveway, they came out of their houses hoping for news about Hattie. His sisters ran to his car. Ruth Ann opened his door. "Ma's gone."

He climbed out of his car. "She's fine. Pa's in the hospital."

Mrs. Randall and Mrs. Lockwood hurried across the street.

He nodded to them. "Our father had a heart attack this morning. Ma's with him at Barrow General."

Lisbeth cried into her hands. He pulled her close. "He's going to be fine."

Ruth Ann stared at her brother. "How do you know?"

He reached for her hand. "Dr. Herschel said he would. Don't worry."

Mrs. Randall said, "I'll make sandwiches for lunch."

Ruth Ann pulled him toward his car. "Take us to the hospital, now."

"Don't leave until I get your lunch ready. Your mother will need to eat." She hurried across the street.

"I'll bring something over for supper. Tell Hattie we're praying for them." Mrs. Lockwood walked to her house.

"Thank you," Victor called after her. "Now, you two, go inside and get ready."

While his sisters dressed for the day, he grabbed his mother's crochet basket and magazines.

He dialed Pastor Lowe's phone number.

"Hello, Pastor Lowe, here."

He wrapped the cord around his finger. "Hey, it's Victor Douglas. Pa had a heart attack this morning. He's at Barrow General."

"I'm very sorry. What room is he in?"

"Room Nine. Can you stop by today?"

"Of course. I can bring Clara with me to sit with Mrs. Douglas."

The last thing his ma needed today was Clara Lowe. "Thank you, but Dr. Herschel said only family can see him, although I'm sure they will make an exception for you."

"Tell your parents, I'll see them this afternoon. Thanks for calling, Victor."

"Thank you, Pastor Lowe." He placed the receiver on the hook. The girls raced down the stairs.

Mrs. Randall knocked on the door and peered through the screen. "Here's your lunch. Let me know if there's anything else I can do."

He took the basket and handed it to Ruth Ann. "Thanks, we will."

He gave the crochet basket and magazines to Lisbeth. "Ready?" He locked the front door as they trudged to the car.

He pulled in front of the hospital and turned the

engine off. Tears streamed down Ruth Ann's face. "Y'all listen. This is hard for you, I know, but Ma needs your strength. She's got enough on her right now. Both of you have to be strong, for her sake. I promise you, Pa will be all right." His voice faded. "He has to be."

Ruth Ann wiped the tears off her face with her hand. "We're okay; aren't we, Lisbeth?"

Lisbeth stared straight ahead and nodded her head.

He helped his sisters out of the car. "He's in room nine. I've got an errand to run."

He watched his sisters walk into the hospital. The gears scraped when he put the car in gear. He maneuvered the old car onto the road and headed to town. He had to tell Dottie about his father before she heard it from someone else.

He walked in the store. Dottie stood over a box stocking shelves. She had on her trousers. He admired how they fit her curves.

She turned. "Hi, may I help you. Oh, Victor, this is a surprise."

"Dottie, I have some bad news. Pa had a heart attack this morning, he's in the hospital."

She walked from behind the counter to where he stood. "Will he be okay?"

"The doctor is giving us hope. I'm not opening the drug store today. I wanted to tell you before you heard the news from someone else."

"Thank you, I'll pray for you and your family. Can I come by tonight?"

"Yes, but only family can go in the room."

"I understand. I'll see you tonight."

****

Victor left his father's room and walked to the

waiting area. Dottie, Ella and Avery sat with the rest of the family. He gave everyone the latest news about Jacob. He shook Avery's hand. "Thanks for bringing Dottie by."

"We hope your father will get well soon. We're here if you need anything."

Dottie followed Avery and Ella to the door.

He took her hand and leaned close. "Can I come by later. I need to talk to you."

"Of course, I'll be waiting for you."

He pulled in front of the boarding house. Standing on the porch, she didn't run to the car like she normally did. She waited at the top of the stairs.

He took her in his arms and kissed the top of her head.

She turned her head. "Victor, I'm so sorry, but he's going to be fine."

"I'm afraid he won't make it."

She shook her head. "Don't say that, he'll make it."

He led her to the bench. "I should have seen this coming." They sat and he turned her face to his. "I know it's late. I needed to see you, to be with you." He took her hand and raised it to his lips. Such softness, her little hand fit inside his fist.

"I'm here for you Victor."

"I don't deserve you." The distance growing between them the last few days melted away. "I'm opening the store tomorrow, so I'll walk you home."

"That would be nice, I missed you today."

They stood and he took her in his arms pressing her entire body as close to his as he could. She initiated the kiss, and his body ached to stay in the embrace. "Thanks for being here."

Dottie stepped back. "This is a difficult time for you and your family."

He turned to go. "I'm going to Frankie's house. I have to let him know."

****

Victor drove his car toward the shanty town. He slowed as he neared the dirt road and avoided as many holes as he could.

He saw a faint light through the window and knocked on the front door.

Frankie glanced out the window before opening the door. "Victor, it's late for you to be out. What's happened?"

He entered and closed the door. He stared at the table surprised, Frankie had been reading his bible. "Pa had a heart attack today. He's in the hospital."

Frankie sat. "How bad?"

"Dr. Herschel says he's going to get over this but he'll need bed rest for a couple of months."

"Anything I can do?"

"Pray."

"I can do that. I'll stop by the hospital tomorrow after work."

He started for the door. "Thanks, Frankie."

Frankie remained seated and picked up his bible. "See you tomorrow."

Chapter Thirty-Five

Victor and Hattie walked into the hospital as the orderlies were delivering breakfast. The heat in the hallway and the disinfectant smell filled his lungs. He walked in his father's room and opened the window.

Hattie rolled the table to the bed. "Good morning, Jacob."

Jacob stirred and opened his eyes. "Morning, Henrietta."

He walked to the end of the bed, pulled out a rod and cranked the head of the bed. "Morning, did you sleep well?"

Jacob put his hand to his face but the oxygen tent stopped him. "Yes, I slept fine."

The nurse came in the room and unzipped the tent so Jacob could eat breakfast. She took the tray from the orderly. "Time for breakfast, Mr. Douglas. Do you need any help?"

Jacob struggled to sit. "No, thank you. I can manage."

Victor caught a glimpse of Dr. Herschel in the hall. He stood by the door waiting.

Dr. Herschel spotted him. "Your father had a restful night. We can only give him oxygen and keep him sedated. I want to send him home in a couple of days. He'll need complete bed rest for eight weeks. If he does well, he can slowly resume his daily activities."

"That's good news, Dr. Herschel. I'll make sure he follows orders this time."

Victor settled his mother in the room and made sure she had enough to keep her busy. "Do you need anything before I go?"

"No, don't worry about us. We'll be fine."

Jacob lowered his cup to his tray trying not to spill his coffee. "Thanks for opening the store, son."

"No problem. I'll see you tonight."

He organized food and prepared for the lunch crowd. All of the business owners on Main Street stopped by to check on Jacob.

At noon the line of people at the lunch counter overwhelmed him. He stood on a chair and yelled above the chatter. "I'm glad to see so many wanting lunch today." The customers shushed each other giving Victor their attention. "The order pad is on the counter. Write what you want and I'll take care of it."

He filled the orders and took money. Every customer thanked him and offered their assistance to the family. At four o'clock, Victor had time to eat. He sat at Jacob's desk and rummaged through the mail for any bills or invoices needing attention. He opened the top drawer and found a letter from a man from Lincolnton, Georgia.

Ned Ayers
Route 2
Lincolnton, Georgia
July 20, 1934

Jacob Douglas
Owner, Douglas Drug Store
109 Main Street
Saplingville, Georgia

Dear Mr. Douglas,

I appreciate the kind offer, and after much deliberation I have decided to go into business with you. As you know, since I graduated pharmacy school I've been working for a local pharmacy here in town, but my dream has always been to have my own place. I recognize you will own sixty percent of the business, and I will own forty percent. That is understandable since you started the business yourself many years ago. I propose we get a lawyer to draw up the papers. Let me know if you have a lawyer or if I should retain one here. I'm hoping our business venture will work favorably, and when you are ready to retire, you will consider selling me your sixty percent share. I also look forward to working with you and learning from your many years of experience and vast knowledge of medicine.

Yours truly,
Ned Ayers

Ned Ayers
Doctor of Pharmacy

Victor settled in his chair and read the letter a second time. He didn't know whether to laugh or cry. Jacob made plans to take care of the business. His heart beat faster. His father was very sick, he would never sell any part of his business. He searched the drawers of the desk. He found no other correspondence from Mr. Ayers. He would wait until Jacob felt better to mention it.

He pushed his chair from the desk and stared at the store shelves. His brain ping ponged what if's. *What if I get the job and Pa still needs me here? What if Pa doesn't recover? I can't leave Ma and two young daughters alone.* Yesterday, he'd been excited and hoped the two weeks would pass by quickly, but now he wished he had more time. At least he had until September when training would start.

He cleaned the store and locked the doors. He walked over to the Five and Dime as Dottie came out the door. "I drove in today; do you want to ride with me to the hospital before I take you home."

"Yes, thank you."

"I had a busy day. The entire town came in for lunch. Everyone asked about Pa. We sold more today than we did last week."

"Well that explains why we were slow, everyone spent their money at the drug store."

He parked his car on the street in front of the hospital. His sisters sat outside on the cement wall. He got out of his car and hurried to the entrance. "How is he today?"

Ruth Ann hugged him. "They say he's better. I hate to see him lying in bed under an oxygen tent."

He kissed the top of her head. "I know you do."

Victor went in the hospital and left Dottie with Ruth Ann and Lisbeth. He walked to the nurse's desk where Dr. Herschel studied a chart. "How's my father? Any improvement?"

Dr. Herschel signed his name on a piece of paper and gave Victor his attention. "Some, he's a strong willed man. I plan to take him off the oxygen tomorrow, and if he doesn't get any worse we're sending him home. Jacob will regain his strength quicker with Henrietta's cooking. He must have complete bed rest. I'll come by the house as often as I need to."

"Thank you, Dr. Herschel."

"There's not much we can do for a heart attack except bed rest. He doesn't smoke, does he?"

"No, he never has that I know of."

Dr. Herschel clutched a chart. "Good, one good thing in his favor. Walk with me."

Victor followed him.

"Are there stairs in your home?"

"Yes, the bedrooms are upstairs."

"You need to put a bed downstairs. He won't be climbing stairs for a while." Dr. Herschel stopped at room fourteen.

"I can do that. I'll have everything ready tomorrow."

"Thanks, Victor." The doctor put his hand on his shoulder. "He's lucky to have a son like you."

"Thanks, Dr. Herschel. I appreciate all you've done." He walked to his father's room. Guilt rose from his stomach like bile. The only way he could be a good son would be to stay in Saplingville.

He pushed the door open and peeked in. Hattie sat in a chair by the bed with her eyes closed. "Ma, you awake?"

"Yes, just saying a prayer."

He entered the room and told her what Dr. Herschel said.

His mother hugged him. "That's great news. I'll take better care of him at home."

He leaned against the wall. "I'm going to ask Frankie to help me move the bed to the living room. We may have to move some furniture."

Hattie took Jacob's hand. "Do whatever you have to."

Victor took Dottie to the boarding house. He motioned for her to sit on the porch bench. He put his arm around her. "Thanks for caring about my family."

She snuggled her head on his shoulder. "I care about you Victor, of course I care about your family."

He cared about her. More than he wanted to admit. He opened his mouth to tell her, but the words wouldn't come. Instead of telling her what she meant to him, he said, "They like you, you fit in."

She lowered her voice. "I didn't at first."

"Well, you do now."

"I…" She stopped. "I'm glad they like me."

He knew she had more to say, he stopped her. "We're bringing Pa home tomorrow. I'll come by and see you in the afternoon."

"I'll be here, let me know if you need help with anything."

Chapter Thirty-Six

Frankie sat in the passenger seat. "Well this isn't how we planned to spend our Saturday, but I'm glad I can help you."

Victor studied the sky. "It's cloudy. I hope the rain holds off until they get him home."

He turned his car into the gravel driveway of the white two story house. He opened the front door and stepped aside for Frankie to enter.

Victor walked in the living room and Frankie leaned on the door jamb. "What do we need to do first?"

He contemplated the parlor. "I'd like to leave the radio and a comfortable chair for Ma. Of course we can't move the piano. We'll take the sofa and other chairs to the bedroom when we disassemble the bed."

They had everything in order in no time. He appreciated his sister's help. They put clean sheets on the bed and fluffed the pillows.

Ruth Ann stood on her tip toes and gave Frankie a hug. "Thanks for helping us."

Frankie slowly put his arms around her. "Glad I could help."

Victor watched the scene out of the corner of his eye. His best friend's face glowed red. "Yeah, Frankie. I couldn't have done this without you. No way I could carry this furniture up and down steps. You're a good fella, thanks."

Frankie stared at the only people who came close to family. "No problem."

The ambulance arrived. The attendants brought Jacob in on a stretcher.

Hattie stood in the door to the living room. "Seems like we have everything we need."

The attendants settled Jacob in bed and turned to leave. "If you need anything, call us."

Victor herded everyone to the kitchen except his ma. "Let's see what the neighbors brought us to eat."

****

Victor stopped by the Boarding House after taking Frankie home. He smelled rain, thunder sounded in the distance. The front door stood open but he knocked on the screen door. Ella kept the doors unlocked all day but he wasn't a boarder and didn't feel comfortable walking in unannounced.

Dottie opened the screen and walked out on the porch. "Victor, did Mr. Douglas go home today?"

"Yeah, he's resting." They sat on the swing. Victor kept the seat at a gentle sway. "How many years did you take care of your mother?"

"Three, but the last six months were the worst. When the doctors told us she only had a few months to live, Daddy started drinking heavy. I served as her care giver and I cherish every moment we spent together. I stood right beside her when she died."

"That's a lot for anyone to bear. You're the strongest girl I've ever met."

"You do what you have to do. I'm glad Mr. Douglas is getting better."

"If he does what Dr. Herschel says, he'll be fine.

The hard part will be to keep him resting for eight weeks."

She scooted closer to him. "At least Mr. Douglas is practically a Doctor himself, so he knows what he has to do to get well."

"He knew the symptoms of a heart attack. Dr. Herschel said it saved him. Some people don't live through a heart attack, they don't understand what's happening. The sooner you get to the hospital, the better chance of recovery."

"That, and you and Mrs. Douglas were there."

He pulled her hand into his lap. "Dottie, I understand what you went through. I feel guilty because my father lived and your mother didn't."

"You shouldn't feel guilty. Mama told me when she got sick she believed everyone has a time to be born and a time to die. She said it was her time, and I shouldn't feel sad. Of course I did. I still feel sad but she's in heaven waiting for us." A gust of air blew her dress. She tucked the material under her legs.

"Sounds like she was a fine Christian woman."

"She told me when I was born she decided to live a life that would be an example for me to follow."

"She certainly did." He pulled her hand to his lips and kissed it. "I've got to get home and check on Pa. We're in for another storm tonight. I'll see you at church tomorrow?"

"Daddy's going with us."

He pulled her into his arms. "Glad to hear that." He gave her a gentle kiss on the mouth and headed home.

****

Sunday morning Victor drove his sisters to church. He sat on their pew watching for Dottie. She arrived with Avery and Ella. He greeted them and led them to the Douglas pew. Frankie came in the church and he motioned for him to sit with them. Frankie's face lit up when he spotted the empty seat next to Ruth Ann. Pastor Lowe asked Victor to give an update on Mr. Douglas' health. He returned to his seat and the preacher said a special prayer for his father's healing. After church, he invited his friends to the house for lunch, but asked they stay quiet.

If Jacob heard a lot of people in the house he would want to visit. When they arrived, Aunt Delores commanded the kitchen. She took her dishes out of the box and heated food the neighbors and friends brought over. He fixed his father a plate and told his mother to eat and visit with everyone.

He joined his pa for Sunday dinner in the living room. "I'm glad to see you feeling better."

Jacob took his plate. "I'm happy to be home, but all I do is sleep and eat."

"Well, that's what you need to do right now." He settled in his chair and started eating.

"Victor, you're doing a great job taking care of us. I appreciate everything."

"No problem, Pa. I'm glad I can be here for you."

They finished their lunch and Hattie brought dessert to share with Jacob.

He stood to give his ma a seat. "Dottie and I are going out. I'll see you a little later."

Hattie took Jacob's plate and gave him a fresh one with cake and pie. "Have a good time."

He went to the kitchen and whispered to Dottie. "Let's go for a ride."

"Where are we going?"

"Out to the lake to feed the ducks. Put some bread in a sack, I'll be right back."

He grabbed a quilt from his bedroom.

He settled Dottie in her seat and backed the car out of the driveway and headed to Uncle Walter's lake. He parked his car on the side of the road as close to the lake as he could.

He guided her to the large oak tree and together they placed the quilt on the ground. "See, right on time to feed the ducks." Victor nodded toward the lake.

Dottie turned, a family of ducks paddled toward them. She grabbed the bag. "Let's go."

They walked to the edge of the lake and threw bread on the ground. The ducks swam ashore.

She giggled and stepped aside when the ducks started fighting over the crumbs. He pulled her close. "They won't hurt you. Here give them the rest of the bread."

She threw the food in all directions and the ducks scattered to get a piece. "We should have brought more bread."

They settled on the quilt. The ducks followed them and waited for more food. One by one they headed to the lake. Occasionally a fish would jump out of the water and the ducks would swim toward the splash.

He relaxed and pulled her close. "What a week."

She leaned into him. "That's an understatement. Are you opening the drug store Monday?"

"I am. I found a letter from a young pharmacist to my father. Pa's been communicating with him about selling forty percent ownership, making him a partner in the store."

She rested her hand on his leg. "He never

mentioned it to you?"

"No, he must have known he wouldn't be able to run the drug store alone. I feel guilty about our arguments."

"Mr. Douglas made plans to bring someone in. He's proud of you and he wants you to succeed."

"I hope you're right, I feel like I may have caused his heart attack." He put his face close to her head so he could breathe in the clean fresh smell of her hair.

"You did no such thing." She turned to face him.

"Oh, baby, I've missed you so much." His lips found hers. He pulled her onto the blanket until they lay side by side. She met his frantic kiss with one of her own. Victor groaned and moved his hand over her until he rested it on her breast. She filled every inch of his hand, he rubbed his thumb over her nipple. She shivered at his touch, sucking his bottom lip. He rolled her on her back, his body followed hers. A perfect fit. *Will I ever desire another woman like I do her?* She moved her arms down his back and pulled him closer. His groin ached, becoming painful. He'd yearned for this since he spotted her walking home at dusk under the street light. He wanted this coveted memory to take with him. He knelt above her and reached for his belt.

Dottie opened her eyes and smiled. The face of an angel. He sat, his conscience arguing with his need. *What the hell am I doing?*

She tugged his arm. "Victor, what's wrong?"

He raised her, their bodies sitting side by side. He stared at the lake. "I would never take advantage of you. I got carried away." He cursed himself. *Why did I bring her here?* His selfish impulse to be alone with her almost made him do something he shouldn't. He wanted to spend every moment he could with Dottie. Her finding someone after he left made him sick.

He pulled her so she stood in front of him. Her eyes searched his for an answer he wasn't ready to give. She pulled his head toward her and kissed him. The urge to pull her to the ground filled his senses. Instead, he took her hands and held them to the side. "I guess we better head home, I need to check on Pa."

They folded the quilt. He took it and guided Dottie toward the car. He dropped her at the boarding house, tension and need fighting with his self-control. He walked into a quiet house and found his father asleep. Lisbeth sat beside the bed while his mother cleaned.

He gathered newspapers and helped his ma tidy the house. "Did Pa mention anything to you about getting a business partner?"

"No, what do you mean?"

"I found a letter in his desk from a pharmacist he'd been communicating with. Pa offered him forty percent of the business. He considered slowing down before this happened. Did he say anything to you?"

Hattie sat in the nearest chair. "This is news to me. I had no idea. Let's wait a few days before we mention the letter. He's tired and the medicine keeps him asleep most of the time."

"I agree, let's see how next week goes."

Chapter Thirty-Seven

Victor and Hattie sat in the living room while Dr. Herschel examined Jacob. He had reduced his medicine a couple of days prior and Jacob begged to get out of bed.

Dr. Herschel listened to his heart and checked the legs and feet for swelling. "You must have complete bed rest for a total of eight weeks then you can slowly start your daily activities. Slowly means you can work half days, but no more."

"I want to at least sit in my favorite chair. I feel like an invalid."

The doctor shook his head. "Jacob, you of all people know what you have to do to get better."

"Yes, I know the protocol for heart attack patients." Jacob smoothed the sheet over his chest.

Dr. Herschel put his stethoscope in his bag. "Yes, I figured you did. My advice is to do what I say, and you shouldn't have any problems."

Jacob extended his hand. "Thanks, Dr. Herschel."

Dr. Herschel shook his hand. "Glad to see you're doing better."

Victor stood and shook Dr. Herschel's hand. "Thanks, doctor."

"I'll be back in a few days. Call me if you need me."

He stayed in the living room while Hattie walked

the doctor out. "Can I get you anything, Pa?"

Jacob became agitated. "I need to talk to you about something. I've been communicating with a Mr. Ayers."

He grabbed some pillows and helped his father sit. "I know, I found the letter when I checked your desk for outstanding bills. I'm sorry for meddling in your business."

Jacob settled against the pillows. "No problem, you need to take care of things. You're doing an outstanding job. Anyway, I never answered his letter. I wanted to give you the store, but you have other plans. What is your take on me getting a business partner?"

He sat next to the bed. "Under the circumstances this is the only way. If you bring in a younger man who can work the long hours needed to run the pharmacy, you can work part time. You'll still have a majority stake in the business, and have someone to run the drug store when you aren't there."

"I've worked six days a week, ten hour days since I opened the drug store twenty-nine years ago. I need to slow down."

"I agree. Do you want me to handle the communication?"

"Yes, ask my lawyer Mr. Peek to answer the letter and ask Mr. Ayers when he can start. You and Mr. Peek can work out the figures, I'll sign whatever papers we need to get this started."

"Don't worry, I'll take care of everything. You concentrate on getting better so you can go to work. You'll never be happy staying home."

"You're right. Good night, son."

"Night, Pa."

He sat on the front porch watching fire flies. Not many years had passed since he and Frankie caught them and put them in jars. They sat the jars on the night table and watched them until they fell asleep.

One problem's solved. Pa planned ahead and found someone. He'd broken up with other girls. The break-ups were hard, but everything always turned out fine. His old girl friends were happily married now. He didn't miss them. Maybe the break with her would be smooth. He just kidded himself. The only thing on his mind since he met her was making whoopee. He would make tracks before it was too late. He had to, for both their sakes. The passion in her kisses, proved she'd gotten too close. He headed upstairs to his room and made plans to blow her off.

Chapter Thirty-Eight

Victor dressed in his best suit and drove to Main Street to meet with Mr. Ayers and Mr. Peek regarding the legal matter of the drugstore partnership.

A secretary took him to Mr. Peek's office. The lawyer stood and shook his hand. "Victor Douglas, Ned Ayers."

"Pleased to meet you. You can call me Victor."

"And please call me Ned." Ned rose from his chair to shake his hand.

He studied the stranger's face. He expected an older man.

"Have a seat, please." Mr. Peek gathered the paperwork and placed a check mark where Mr. Douglas needed to sign. "Have your father sign these and bring them to me tomorrow."

He read through the papers. "I believe everything's in order. Ned, would you like to come with me so you can meet my father?"

"Yes, I would like to very much."

They walked to his car. "Where are you staying?"

"Where do you recommend?"

"I have a friend who runs a boarding house. It's nothing fancy but you get a room and a hot meal on Sunday."

"Just what I need until I can find a place to rent or buy. Is it near enough to town so I can walk to work?"

"As a matter of fact it is. I'll take you there after you meet my father."

****

After introducing Ned to Jacob and both signing papers to get the partnership going, Victor dropped Ned off at the boarding house. According to the papers, Ned was a year older than him. He glared at Ned as he sauntered toward the house. Ned was a nice looking man, alone in a new town. Dottie would be available soon. His hands gripped the steering wheel. Miss Simons opened the door and Ned shook her hand. He started his car and turned toward home.

The next morning he showed Ned around the store when Dottie walked by on her way to work.

Ned strolled to the window. "Man, she's the bee's knees. Lucky me, she lives at the boarding house. We met last night."

Victor continued to work. "She's my girl."

"Sorry man, I didn't know. Thought you were leaving town. Are you engaged to be married?"

He clenched his fists. He wanted to punch the handsome Ned in the nose. The realization of what would happen to Dottie when he left, and who her next boyfriend would be stared him in the face. "No, we aren't engaged."

Ned turned. "Oh, I see."

He changed the subject and continued telling Ned about the store. Ned greeted customers and filled prescriptions, while he ran the lunch counter, cleaned and stocked shelves. He fumed about Ned's comments all day. He would make sure Ned watched him walk Dottie home. The two of them living in the same house made his blood boil.

Victor locked the door to the store. He said goodbye to Ned and strolled over to the Five and Dime.

Ned walked ahead of them. He turned and stopped walking waiting for them. "Hi Dottie, did you have a good day at work?"

"I did. How do you like your new job?" She gave him her full attention.

"I love the store. Victor's giving me the low down." Ned fell into step with them toward the boarding house.

He stared at Ned and Dottie carrying on like old friends. As soon as he left this man would step in. She and Ned continued laughing and talking. He reached for her hand. He held it the rest of the way.

He opened the screen door. Ned waited for Dottie to enter. Victor pulled her close. "See you in the morning, Ned."

Ned hesitated then nodded and entered the boarding house.

He grabbed her placing a rough kiss on her lips.

She pushed him away and whispered. "Everyone can see us."

He glared through the screen. He turned her face toward him. "I'll see you tomorrow."

He walked home in a fit of rage and regret. Ned was becoming a pill. He ate supper and went to Frankie's house.

He parked the car and joined Frankie on the front porch. "How are you?"

Frankie pulled a chair out for him. "Good, how's Mr. Douglas?"

"He's fine. He feels like reading now. Ma's going to the library every day, and he's listening to the radio.

His appetite's improved." Victor sat in the straight chair and leaned against the wall.

"Has the new business partner arrived?"

"Oh, yeah he's here." He plopped the chair hard on the porch and stood.

"You don't sound very happy. Thought you'd be overjoyed to leave the drudgery behind." Frankie stood and faced him.

"I'm happy for my father."

"Yeah, and?"

"He's living at the boarding house." He pulled the chair close to the rail and sat.

"That's what people do when they get into town, and have no place else to go, so?" Frankie stepped into the yard peering over the rail.

"He's young and handsome…and single." He put his head in his hands.

"Uh huh, so is Dottie. I see your point. But Victor, you knew this was bound to happen. All the other dames you dumped found someone else. Don't you want her to be happy?"

"Well, yeah, I do." Victor stood.

"You're leaving and you don't want to take her with you. You gotta make up your mind, man."

He inspected the sky. "You know what a pilot's life is like. I don't have a choice. I'm not taking her with me."

"Well, you've got to leave her behind. Get over it." Frankie sat in his chair.

Victor turned. "You're right. When I'm gone, I won't have to see them together."

"What makes you think they'll be together? There are other young men in this town, present company included." Frankie put his feet on the rail.

"Well I know for a fact, you only have eyes for one girl in this town."

Frankie said softly, "Lot of good that does me."

Victor lowered his head. "We're in the same boat my friend."

He said good-bye to Frankie and drove straight to the boarding house. He parked the car and marched to the porch. Avery, Ella, Dottie, and Ned were laughing and talking. Avery and Ella said hello and went in the house. Ned sat in his chair like a fly stuck in honey.

He glowered at the man. "I'd like to talk to Dottie."

"Okay, I'm not stopping you."

"I mean, privately."

Ned walked toward the front door. "Oh, sure, see you later."

Dottie frowned. "That was rude."

He lowered his head and locked eyes with her. "You are my girl."

"Oh, really? I'm your girl when it's convenient for you. I'm yours until you jump in your plane and ride off in the clouds, then what. Then what, Victor?"

He turned and walked to the porch rail. "I'm sorry I can't stand the thought of you with anyone but me."

"Ned's a friend, he's new in town and we're trying to make him feel at home. Nothing more."

He wanted to grab her, stake his claim. Instead he turned to face her. "I'm sorry. I'll see you tomorrow."

****

Victor could kick himself for being such a twit. He didn't want to cause any trouble between his father and Ned. They were business partners. He needed to act professional but he expected Ned would make his move on his girl after he left. Ned, a lonely bachelor ready to settle down and Dottie conveniently here. He could see her life falling into place. He arrived home. He locked the front door. Peeking into the living room he found his parents asleep together, his mother's head on his father's chest. He smiled and took the stairs two at a time. He turned on his desk lamp and stared at the blue envelope. He grabbed his letter opener, slicing the envelope open.

Mr. Morton Posey
Delta Air Corporation
Candler Field
Post Office Box 105
Atlanta, Georgia
August 15, 1934

Victor Douglas
283 Vine Street
Saplingville, Georgia
Dear Mr. Douglas,

We are pleased to announce, you have been selected for a position as a Delta Airlines Pilot. Your training will begin on Monday, September 10, 1934 at 8:00am. Please arrive in Atlanta on Saturday, September 8, by noon. We have reserved a block of rooms at a nearby hotel for you and your fellow pilots. There will be a brief orientation Saturday afternoon, then you will be taken to the hotel to settle in until Monday morning.

I look forward to seeing you.
Sincerely,
M. Posey

Morton Posey
Hiring Manager

Delta Air Corporation

He sat at his desk and read the letter several times. The dream he'd kept for so long came true tonight. He needn't worry about the drug store. He'd given the Jenny to Frankie. Ned had blown into town ready to step in as Dottie's boyfriend. The restraints were gone. He should be the happiest man on earth.

****

Victor arrived at the drug store as Ned unlocked the front door.

Ned stepped aside to allow him to come in. "I'm sorry if I offended you last night. We were all having fun, telling stories about where we grew up. I didn't know you were serious about Dottie."

He took a deep breath. He didn't want to cause any trouble before he left. "I told you she's my girl. I needed to talk to her about something."

"Well whatever you said upset her. I heard her crying after you left."

His face stung as if he'd been slapped. He hadn't told anyone about his letter, he wanted to tell Dottie first. Why did he feel like she'd be doing a lot more crying tonight, and who would be there to console her? He had to clear his mind and get to work. He would be civil to this man, for his family's sake.

He faced Ned. "I'm sorry too. I've been under a lot of stress lately with my family. I'll talk to Dottie this afternoon and straighten everything out."

Straighten everything out, bull shit. He'd dreaded this since the first day he caught a glimpse of her walking down the sidewalk. He didn't expect to care this much. He would take her to the lake and tell her as they sat under the oak tree.

She'd be upset, it would give her time to cry and accept the break-up before he took her home. He certainly didn't want to tell her at home, Avery might come out swinging for his baby girl. Ned would probably join in too. A brawl was all he needed. No, the oak tree and lake were a special place. He'd rather remember their days kissing and holding each other there. He needed a place they'd never been before. Spangler Park, built by the Cotton Mill for the town. Perfect. There were plenty of benches situated away from the swings and slides. They would have privacy.

The workday ended and he waited for Dottie outside the Five and Dime.

She wouldn't meet his eyes. "I wasn't sure you'd be here today."

He walked beside her keeping a safe distance. "Why?"

"Well, after last night, I figured you would be mad."

He pulled her hand to his mouth and kissed it, "No, you should be angry. I had no cause to do what I did."

She studied his eyes trying to read them. "You're forgiven."

He licked his lips. "I need to talk to you tonight. I'll be here at seven."

"Sure, I'll be ready. Where are we going?"

"To the park."

"I'd love to." Dottie watched him walk toward the street. He turned and she waved and smiled.

He arrived home, entering through the back door. "Ma, I won't be here for supper."

Hattie stood at the counter peeling potatoes. "You and Dottie going out to eat?"

"No. Just taking her to the park. She's never been there."

"I see." Hattie rinsed the potatoes in the sink. "I'll leave something on the stove in case you're hungry later."

She didn't mention the letter, and he didn't offer any news. His stomach churned and his hands were sweaty. The feeling reminded him of his first training exercise. He'd rather face an enemy in the bomber, than break the news to Dottie.

He sat in his room rereading the letter from Mr. Posey. At five minutes before seven he headed to his car.

Chapter Thirty-Nine

Victor got out of his car and walked toward the steps to the boarding house. Dottie stood at the porch rail wearing her trousers. *God, she's gorgeous in those pants. Did she have to wear them tonight?*

She barreled down the stairs. "Ready."

He smiled. "Yes, you are. You are lovely tonight Miss Lester."

"Well Mr. Douglas, it's not every day a girl has a date during the week."

He opened the car door and helped her inside. Now he knew how Uncle Walter feels when he kills one of his pigs. He knows he has to do it but he doesn't want to.

Dottie waited until he guided the car away from the curb. "I've never been to this park."

He stopped at a stop sign and faced her. "Spangler Cotton Mill built it for their employees, but the entire town uses it. They have swings and sliding boards for kids. They even built an all-purpose building used for public gatherings and parties."

He turned right and headed to the park. He couldn't do it, he would wait until another day. His family and Uncle Walter flashed before his eyes, he had to tell them. He parked the car and led her to a bench away from the playground. He didn't want kids interfering with their visit.

He took Dottie's hand, brought it to his lips and kissed it. He closed his eyes, lingering, memorizing the taste of her. He rested on the bench, remembering the reason for their date. "I like those trousers on you."

"A nice young gentleman bought them." She reached over and placed her other hand on his. You've done so much for me and my daddy. I want to thank you again for helping. He's been a changed man since the night you found me trying to get him home. I couldn't handle him, had just about given up when you drove by."

"A situation like that takes a man to man conversation to straighten things out."

"You opened his eyes. He's been a better man since."

"Well, Ella should take some credit."

"They're getting close, and I'm glad they have each other. She's been good to me, too."

He put his arm around her. "How's the new boarder working out?"

"Ned?"

"Yes, Ned."

"He's a nice man. He's like all of us living there. He's in transition. He wants to find a house to rent or buy. He said he really likes the drug store, and loves the town's people. He can't wait to work with Mr. Douglas. Says he wants to learn all he can from an expert. "Is that why you brought me here, so you didn't have to share me?"

"In a way. I need to talk to you alone and don't want any distractions."

She smiled and her eyes locked with his. "Well, here I am."

He pulled her close and kissed her square on the mouth, his tongue searching. If this was the last time, he'd damn well do it right.

She pushed him. "Victor's there's too many people."

He took both her hands in his. "Dottie, I got the job."

She blinked. "Victor, this is what you always wanted. I'm happy for you."

He wiped the lone tear drop from her face. "I'm so sorry. We've had a great time. You're very special. I'll never forget you."

Dottie stood. "Please take me home."

He moved toward the car, but the parking lot might as well have been miles. He had a sensation of sloshing through waist deep water. He reached for her hand. She pulled it away.

What did she expect? He'd told her his plans from the start of their relationship. This wasn't his fault. He watched Dottie. She walked a step ahead of him, her back straight, staring ahead. She did a good job keeping her feelings hidden.

Ned would tell him tomorrow how she cried all night in her room. The last thing he wanted to hear. Ned would swoop in, and take care of everything. No doubt about that. He would get over this summer romance. Nothing he hadn't done before. He opened the car door for her and walked to the driver's side.

When he settled in his seat, she faced him. "Victor, I'm happy for you, this is what you've dreamed of all your life. I don't want us to part as enemies. You've been the nicest man I've ever known. I'll miss you."

He almost sobbed out loud. She was a lady, her

mama taught her well. "No Dottie, never enemies, always friends."

Silence filled the air. He tried to make small talk, but he couldn't find any words.

When he parked the car, she turned toward the side window. "Please don't get out. I'll get myself in."

He watched her sit with Ella on the front porch bench before he pulled out into the street.

Ella scooted over to give her room. "Why didn't Victor come in, is Mr. Douglas okay?"

Dottie took a deep breath. "Yes, Mr. Douglas is fine. We broke-up. He got the job."

"Oh, honey, I'm so sorry. I hoped things would work out for you two. That man loves you more than he'll admit."

"He doesn't love me. I thought we had something but we don't. I'm a stupid girl."

"If he isn't the one for you someone better will come along."

"That's what Mama used to tell me."

"Never give up, Dottie. Don't let this bad break leave you bitter."

"I won't, but getting over Victor will take time." Dottie wiped tears off her face with the back of her hand.

Chapter Forty

Victor drove to his uncle's house. Uncle Walter, his rock and confidant listened, and gave advice. He needed some tonight.

He parked his car. His uncle sat in his rocker, the old dog asleep on the floor close beside him. Victor sat in the car afraid to get out.

Walter stood and walked to the porch rail. "Is everything all right at home?"

He exited his car and rambled to the porch. "Yes, everyone's fine. Your sister's enjoying taking care of her husband. She has a new reason to get up in the morning.

Walter nodded. "That's Hattie, all right. Always loves a challenge. What's on your mind?"

"I wanted to tell you I got the job. I start training September tenth."

"I didn't have a doubt for one minute."

"You're the second person I've told." He walked to the porch beam, stretched his arms overhead and pulled until his back popped.

"Who was the first?"

"Dottie."

"How'd it go?" Walter settled in his rocker.

"Not good, well it went better than I thought. She's such a lady, she appeared to take the break-up well, but I could tell she didn't." Victor paced back and forth.

"How do you feel?"

"What do you mean?" He stood still.

"I mean, I thought you were getting close. I've never seen you as attentive, and caring toward any of your other girlfriends. Delores and I hoped she'd be the one for you."

He sat in the rocker. "Yeah, I really liked her too."

"But you aren't in love with her?" Walter stared straight ahead.

He regarded the large oak tree in the front yard while he put his words together. "Yes, right, I'm not in love. At least, I don't believe I am. I care more for her than any girl I've dated. I really don't have anything to compare my feelings to. I've never been in love before."

Walter put his hand on his arm. "Your heart will tell you when you're in love. Listen to it. Don't live a lifetime of regret wondering what would have happened if."

He stood to leave, and hugged his uncle. "Thanks for everything."

Walter returned the hug. "You bet."

He had one more stop to make on the way home. Frankie would be happy to get his Jenny back. He parked and walked to the front porch. Frankie sat on the porch reading by the light of a kerosene lamp. "Are you reading a book?"

Frankie dog-eared the page. "I told you I'd been studying. Right now I'm reading *Lost Horizon* by James Hilton. The book is about…"

Victor interrupted, "Yeah, I know what it's about. A place where life is lived in peace away from the troubles the rest of us live in. Shangri-La doesn't exist."

Frankie put his book on the table next to the lamp. "Who put a bee in your bonnet?"

"No one. I came to tell you I got the job." He leaned against the two by four.

"Well, don't sound so happy about it."

"I'm happy about the job."

"You told her, didn't you? You told Dottie and you broke it off."

"There wasn't anything to break off. We had some good times, that's it." He turned and stared at the field across the street.

"Man, she really got to you. A girl finally penetrated Victor Douglas' heart. Never thought I'd see the day."

He glared at Frankie. "You ain't seen nothing. She's okay with it, and I am too."

"Well good, I'd hate to see you make a wrong choice, and screw your life up."

"I'm good, the only bad choice I made was staying here as long as I did." He crossed his arms.

Frankie stood. "I'm sorry if you got sidetracked with us country bumpkins."

He raised his hands. "That's not what I meant. You know you're my best friend and always will be."

Frankie cleared his throat. "I know, let's don't get teary eyed or anything."

"I really hope things work out for you Frankie, take care of our Jenny. I hope you can make some extra money with the plane. I'll see you before I go."

"You'd better not leave town without saying goodbye."

He walked to his car. "Take care, Frankie."

He headed home to tell his family. He'd need to get

in a better mood, before he told them. His mother could read his mind. In all of his twenty-four years, he'd never fooled her.

He found everyone in the living room, listening to the radio. He put a big smile on his face. "I have great news. I got the job. I have to be in Atlanta on Saturday, September eighth."

His sisters hugged him. He grabbed them and whirled them around.

Ruth Ann said, "My brother's going to be an airline pilot."

Lisbeth broke free and steadied herself. "Maybe you can fly us somewhere for a vacation when Pa gets better."

Hattie stood and took her son's face in her hands. He bent. She kissed his forehead. "I am so proud of you."

He walked over to the bed.

Jacob shook his hand. "Congratulations, son."

Ruth Ann twirled. "Can we plan a going away party?"

Hattie nodded. "Yes, we'll ask Aunt Delores if we can have the party there. The doctor doesn't want your father to get excited, or have too many visitors. Jacob and I will have to miss the party, but we'll be there in spirit."

He stared at his family, a stab of regret settled in his bones. "I hate to leave you."

Hattie regarded her son. "Nonsense, we're fine. Jacob's getting better every day."

Jacob grunted, "The doctor doesn't know what he's talking about. I'm perfectly fine. He's making me a prisoner in my own home. You go on, and don't worry about us. Ned seems to be doing a good job at the drugstore. Tell him to find someone to take over your job."

"I will."

"Come in the kitchen and I'll get your food," Hattie said as she walked toward the door.

He followed her to the kitchen and sat.

She placed his plate on the table. "Have you told Dottie?"

"Yes, I told her first."

"She's a sweet girl, Victor. I hope she wasn't upset."

"A little, but she understood. I've told her from the beginning what my plans were."

"How do you feel about never seeing her again? I had the feeling you were getting close." She put his tea glass beside his bowl.

"I'm fine. I would have liked to get to know her better, but there wasn't enough time."

Hattie sat in the chair opposite him. "I don't want you regretting anything later down the road."

Suddenly the vegetable soup didn't seem as appetizing. "I won't; don't worry."

Chapter Forty-One

Victor and Frankie spent the weekend working on the Jenny and flying. He settled in the front seat and let his dare devil friend take the controls. The bi-plane belonged to him now. They talked with Walter about Frankie crop dusting and giving flying lessons. Hearing them make plans made him home sick, and he hadn't even left.

When they got in the car and headed home, a hush filled the air. Frankie broke the silence. "Do you feel better about leaving? I got the impression you weren't too happy."

"I can't wait to fly the new ships."

Frankie laughed. "Well, as they say, if you can fly a Jenny, you can fly anything."

"I've heard that before. The saying should be, if you can land a Jenny, you can land anything."

They both laughed.

He slowed the car and made a right turn on the highway, the gears ground as he pushed the clutch in. "Did you ever want to be a commercial pilot?"

Frankie shook his head. "Not for me. I want to fly, but to me a commercial pilot is no more than a glorified bus driver, going from one place to another. Too restricting. Besides, as ratty as my little house is, I'm a homebody. I don't want to travel. When the sun goes down, I want my head on my pillow in my bed."

"So what is your dream?"

Frankie thought for a moment. "My dream is working at a small airport. I'd like to teach flying, take people for rides, and do some crop dusting. I like to work with my hands, so I'd like to be a mechanic on other people's planes."

"Hope it works out for you. You'll need to move to a town with a small airport." Victor turned off the highway onto a dirt road.

"That's my plan."

Victor pulled the car into Frankie's front yard. "I'll give you a good reference, and I know Uncle Walter will."

Frankie stepped out of the car and leaned his tall frame toward the window of the car. "Thanks, Victor."

Victor backed his car into the road and waved. He had a sick feeling in his stomach. It reminded him of the time he broke Mrs. Howard's lamp, and he and Frankie ran out to play without telling her. Frankie took all the blame and got a good whipping. This guilty feeling was worse because he was older, and knew better.

****

Victor unlocked the front door of the drug store. Dottie and Ned walked toward him. She smiled and they talked like bosom buddies. He should have been happy to see her smile, but his face heated and his pulse quickened. He gripped the edge of a shelf willing himself not to run out and pull her in his arms. He turned and walked to the lunch counter.

Ned strolled in the drug store. "Good morning."

He wiped the counter. "Good morning to you. How was your Sunday, did you do anything special?"

"No, I try to rest on Sunday and get ready for the work week. How's Mr. Douglas?"

He busied himself at the sink. "He's getting better every day. He's tired of bed rest. I wouldn't be surprised if he didn't find a cure for heart attack patients."

Ned opened a bottle and started counting pills. "I wouldn't either; he's a very smart man. He should have been a doctor instead of a pharmacist."

"I agree," Victor said as he organized food for sandwiches. He wanted to ask about Dottie, but decided to keep those thoughts to himself. "Pa said to tell you to find someone to take my place. I'll be gone in a few weeks, and unless you want to feed the lunch crowd and dispense medicine, you need to find someone."

"I'll start the search. Do I need to get hiring permission from Mr. Douglas?"

"No, he said you make the decision."

Ned nodded his head. "I appreciate the trust."

Chapter Forty-Two

Dottie surveyed the store. She'd come to love every inch of the Five and Dime. Mr. Murphy said the place shined and credited her for the beautiful displays. Her hands were sweaty, the sensation of quick sand glued her feet to the floor. *One step at a time.* She made it to the back of the store and stood a few feet from his desk. "Mr. Murphy, when you get time, I need to talk to you."

"Sure thing, as soon as I finish this paper work."

Dottie walked to the front, took a bottle of alcohol and a rag and started cleaning the glass cases. The store bustled with customers until two in the afternoon. When the shoppers left the store, she straightened items on the shelves.

Mr. Murphy walked to the front with a box. "What do you need to talk to me about?"

Dottie's stomach turned over. She didn't want to quit her job but she had to get out of Saplingville. She couldn't live here without Victor. "Mr. Murphy, my last day to work for you will be Friday week. I'm moving to Macon to live with my aunt."

Mr. Murphy opened the box and counted the rolls of ribbon before he spoke. "This comes as a surprise. I thought you liked your job."

She couldn't tell him the real reason. "I've got Daddy settled in a job, and he and Ella are becoming more than friends. My mother's sister lives in Macon and she wants me to move there."

"Well, Dottie, I sure will miss you. You're the best help I've ever had. I wish I could change your mind." Mr. Murphy studied her. "Your family's been through a lot in the last year. I'm sure you'll be a comfort to your aunt."

"Will you give me a letter of reference?"

"By all means, whoever hires you will be very lucky."

"Thanks, Mr. Murphy."

She noticed the clock. Ten minutes passed time to leave. She peeked out the window toward the drug store. Victor walked toward his home. Good, she didn't want to see him. She left the store as Ned locked the drug store.

Ned waved and she walked across the street. "Dottie, mind if I walk you home?"

She swallowed hard and took a deep breath. "No, I need someone to talk to. I told Mr. Murphy I was moving."

Ned stopped and put his hands on her shoulders. "Are you sure you want to leave?"

A tear slipped down her cheek. "I can't stay here. Not after. Well, you know."

"I do know and I'm sorry."

Dottie reached into her pocketbook and pulled out a handkerchief to wipe the tears off her face. She walked with Ned in the direction of the boarding house. "Mr. Murphy's the best boss, and I really liked my job."

"I'll bet he's sad to see you go."

"That's what he said."

Ned took Dottie's hand, stopped walking, and turned her to face him. "Are you sure this is what you want to do?"

She took her hand from him and continued walking. "This is what I have to do. I need to be on my own. Aunt Bess will let me live with her until I can find a place. She misses Mama, and she needs me. Daddy said he'll drive me to Macon. I'd appreciate you not saying anything to anyone in town."

"I understand, I won't tell anyone."

They walked in silence until they reached the boarding house.

Dottie helped prepare the table for supper. She went to Ned's room and knocked on his door. "Ella made bean soup and cornbread, it's ready if you want some."

Ned opened the door. "Sure, sounds good. I'll be down in a jiffy."

She made her way to the kitchen and poured tea in four glasses.

Avery stood in the kitchen door watching. "Did you tell Mr. Murphy you were quitting?"

Dottie placed two glasses on the table and turned for the others. "I told him."

Avery sat at the head of the table. "What'd he say?"

"He said he hated to see me go."

"I'll bet he does. You're a good employee."

Ned sat in the empty chair. "Boy, this smells good. You're a great cook."

Ella blushed. "Thank you, it's simple food."

Ned took a sip of tea. "Simple's the best, I always say."

Avery said a prayer over the food. He clutched his spoon staring at his daughter. "How 'bout we all go to the picture show tonight?"

Dottie shook her head. "I really don't want to do anything."

Avery crumbled cornbread in his soup. "I insist. Ella, Ned, want to go?"

Ella gave Avery a big smile. "I'd love to."

Ned took a drink of iced tea. "That's a grand idea. How about us men do the dishes while you girls get ready."

She didn't want to disappoint anyone. She'd be gone soon and had no idea when she would see her father again. "Sounds like a good trade off."

Chapter Forty-Three

Victor sat in his room reading *Lone Cowboy* by Will James. Ruth Ann stood in the doorway. "Need something?"

She walked in his room. "Want to go to the picture show with me?"

He turned the page to save his place and closed the book. "Who's going with you?"

"Some friends. Not Anna."

He smiled, their argument about Anna seemed years ago. "I'm gonna stay home and read. Lisbeth might want to go."

"I'll ask her, see you later."

****

Victor spent the evening reading in his room and thinking about moving. He took a pad and pencil out of his desk and wrote a list of things he needed to take with him to Atlanta.

Ruth Ann walked in his room. "Dottie went to the movie with Ned."

He clinched his teeth and swallowed. "That's nice."

"You aren't a little jealous?" She sat on his bed.

"No, she's free to see whoever she wants."

"Why'd you break-up with her? I've never seen you in love with anyone before."

He opened the drawer and placed his list inside.

"I'm not in love."

Ruth Ann ran her fingers through the chenille bedspread. "Could've fooled me."

"I'm leaving in a few weeks." He turned to face his sister. "I'm glad she found someone else."

She searched his face. "Yes, she and Ned make a nice couple."

Ned stepped in. He hoped it would take place after he left. He didn't want to see them together. "I'm glad she found someone so soon."

Ruth Ann walked to the door and turned. "I'm glad it doesn't bother you. I don't want to see you hurt."

He opened the drawer and pulled his book out. "It's not the first time I've broken up with a girl and it won't be the last."

Victor stared at the pages. He had to read over paragraphs several times for the words to sink into his brain.

Chapter Forty-Four

Dottie dressed for work and headed to the front door. Ned stood in the parlor waiting.

He walked to the front door and opened it for her. "I had fun last night."

She walked out the front door. "I had fun too. I'm going to miss this town."

Ned closed the screen door slowly so it wouldn't snap. "Well if Macon doesn't work out maybe you'll come back."

"Maybe. Aunt Bess says there's a business school in Macon. Daddy said he would pay."

"You need a good trade."

"Yes, I'm excited. I wanted to do something after high school, but Mama got sick. Then Daddy's drinking got bad and I had to support him."

"This is your time, Dottie."

They turned on Main Street. They stood on the sidewalk in front of the drug store. She glimpsed through the window, meeting Victor's glare. "Hope you have a good day, Ned. Remember don't say anything about me moving to Macon."

"My lips are sealed."

Ned walked in the door. "Good Morning."

"Morning, Ned." Victor walked toward the lunch counter.

"How's Mr. Douglas today?"

"Much better, thanks."

The two men started their daily duties. Victor walked to the front of the store glancing out the window.

Ned watched him. "Dottie's doing fine."

Victor scowled. "I'm glad she is. I see you two are getting pretty close."

"As close as friends can get."

"That's good, Ned. That's real good."

Chapter Forty-Five

Saturday morning, Victor backed his old car out of the driveway and headed to the shanty town to get Frankie. He drove down the road where the boarding house stood. He slowed and stared at Dottie's window on the second floor. The lace curtain beckoned him. He wished he could take her flying one more time before he left.

They arrived at the farm and walked to the plane shed. "I wanted to help you work on her one more time before I go. I'm going to miss this plane."

Frankie ran his hand along the wing. "She's the steadiest JN-4 I've ever flown. I'll bet you're going to miss more than the Jenny. Have you seen Dottie?"

"No. She's moving on with Ned." He untied the tarp and pulled it off the bi-plane.

"You're jumping to conclusions. When you love someone, you can't turn love off and start with someone else. I know from experience." Frankie climbed on the wheel and peered at the engine.

"I'll be glad when I get out of this town. I won't miss the Jenny because I'll be flying other planes. The same with Dottie, I'll find someone else to fill my time." He handed Frankie the oil can.

"You just can't admit a dame stole your heart."

Victor laughed. "I've never been in love in my life. I admit I liked her more than anyone I've dated but this isn't love."

"You could have fooled me."

"How 'bout you, have you decided where you're going?"

"I'm talking to a friend at the Savannah Municipal Airport about a mechanic job. I can do that while I teach and crop dust." Frankie pulled the chocks out from under each wheel.

"You'll have access to newer airplanes. Maybe they'll let you fly those."

"Yes, I can test fly after I work on them…to make sure they're safe." They pushed the Jenny out to the runway.

"You'll be the first test flying mechanic in history."

Frankie laughed. "If that's what it takes."

Chapter Forty-Six

Dottie sat on the porch staring into space when Ned arrived home. "Did you have many customers today?"

"We're always busy on Saturday, mostly mill people who can't get off during the week. Mind if I join you?"

"No, not at all." She scooted over and made room on the bench.

"Dottie, are you sure you want to move? I'd like for us to get to know each other better."

"Ned, I wish I'd met you first, but I need time to get over Victor."

He took her hand. "I wish you'd met me first too. If you were my girl I would never give you up."

Dottie stared at their hands joined together. No electricity flowed between them. Ned beat Victor in the handsome department. His blond hair and steel blue eyes would make any girl swoon. Victor had an inner strength. She liked his rough edges, and take charge attitude. "Thank you for saying that. I fell in love with the wrong man."

"I'll be here when you finish school. We can see each other then."

"You would wait?"

Ned kissed her on the lips. "I sure would. I know a special girl when I meet one."

The intimacy surprised her. She stared into his blue

eyes. He lowered his head, their lips met again. She deepened their kiss searching for answers. Still no sparks flew. She pulled away. "Ned, you're a handsome and smart man, you'll find someone."

"There aren't many girls like you here."

Dottie took her hand from his. "I guess we'll have to see where the future takes us."

Ned cared the way she wanted Victor to. In a relationship both people should love equally. If her daddy had loved her mama as much as she loved him, he would have never cheated. She should take the easy way, date Ned, and see where it led, but her heart wasn't in it. She wouldn't play with Ned's emotions the way Victor played with hers.

Chapter Forty-Seven

Lisbeth informed Victor his going away party would be Saturday at Uncle Walter's house. Aunt Delores planned enough food for an army and ladies were asked to bring a covered dish. They were going to have a feast.

He didn't ask who they invited, but he hoped Dottie would come with Avery and Ella. He wanted to see her one last time before he left. They might even sneak in a plane ride. No, they could never be just friends.

If he stood within ten feet of her he would be holding her hand or sneaking a kiss. He counted the days until he could leave all this behind. Out of sight, out of mind…he hoped.

He made sure he came to work late and left early. Many times during the week, he wanted to ride or walk by the boarding house to get a glimpse of Dottie.

Ned didn't mention her and he didn't ask. As for the drug store, the young pharmacist did a fine job and the customers liked him. Jacob couldn't have found a better partner.

****

On Saturday morning Victor drove to Uncle Walter's farm with his sisters. They stopped to pick up Frankie. They had a good time laughing and joking. He noticed Ruth Ann was more attentive to Frankie than she'd ever been and Frankie behaved like a perfect gentleman. The summer had changed everyone. They all matured into the people they were destined to be.

They arrived at the farm early to help. Aunt Delores gave orders. Uncle Walter let her run with it. The guests arrived and before long the tables were full of food. Avery and Ella were the last to show, without Dottie. Victor couldn't breathe. It was final. He'd never see her again.

Frankie got everyone's attention and made a speech. "I want to say I am proud to call Victor Douglas my best friend. We've been through lots of stuff together, some good, and some bad, but he always had my back. He left town to go into the United States Army Air Corp. He made us proud of him then. I know he's going to do great things as a commercial pilot. I'll miss you buddy. Best of luck to you."

Walter made the next speech. "I am extremely proud of my nephew, and the man he has grown into. I hoped he would stay here. I offered to give him land to build an airport for our community, but bigger and better things drew his attention."

He watched as his friends and family gasped, and started talking among themselves. They were shocked he would turn down such an offer. A vein in Avery's head twitched. He must be furious with him and how he treated his daughter.

Walter continued, "But a man has to follow his dream. We are pleased Victor found his."

Ruth Ann commented next. "My parents are sorry they can't be here. They are proud of my brother. He returned home after his time in the service to help us and now we have to let him go. We'll miss him."

Everyone started singing, 'For He's The Jolly Good Fellow'. He didn't feel like a jolly good fellow. He realized by leaving he let his family, the town, and Dottie down.

He walked over to Avery and shook his hand. "Thanks for coming. How's Dottie?"

Avery acknowledged him. "Thanks for inviting us. Ella and I wanted to wish you good luck. Dottie's fine, I took her to Macon last night. She's staying with her Aunt Bess. I'm paying tuition for business school."

Gone. The thought of flying around the country and living a solitary life made him sick at his stomach. He wanted to be with Dottie. He loved her.

He grabbed Avery by the shoulders. "What's the address?"

Avery moved Victor's hands. "Dottie gave clear instructions she didn't want to see you again."

"Mr. Lester, I love her, I can't imagine my life without her."

"That's not what she told me." Avery turned and walked off.

He took two steps and grabbed the man's arm. "I've changed my mind."

Avery jerked his arm free. "What about your career?"

"She's more important."

The older man moved closer to him. "Dottie's more important than what?"

He grabbed Avery by his shoulders, his voice getting louder. "My career. I love her. I have to find her."

Dottie's father studied him. "You're going to give up your dream for my baby girl?"

Victor smiled for the first time since the break-up. Peace flowed through his body. Everything became clear. "I'm giving up my dream for Dottie and the love we have. We'll dream bigger dreams together and make them come true."

Avery grabbed Victor's arm. "Do you want me to drive you?"

"No, I can get there quicker in the Jenny. I'll get a ride at the airport to the house."

He wrote the address on a piece of paper. He whispered his plans to Frankie and Uncle Walter. They ran with him to the shed where they went through their safety checks. He took off, and headed to Macon. He figured he could get there and have her in Saplingville within a couple of hours. He watched the men take off their hats and the women shade their eyes as they watched the Jenny fly above them.

He arrived at Miller Field in Macon and took a taxi to Bess' house. He knocked on the door and a beautiful middle aged lady opened it. "Are you Aunt Bess?" He pulled out his comb and smoothed his hair.

Bess smiled at the good looking man. "Well, that's what my niece calls me. Who are you?"

"I'm Victor Douglas, and I'm here to see Dottie."

Bess pushed the screen door open. "I'll get her. Come in and make yourself comfortable."

He couldn't sit. He stood at the window rattling the change in his pocket.

Dottie walked in the living room and glared at him. "What are you doing here?"

He walked toward her. "Mr. Lester told me where you were. Why didn't you tell me you were leaving?"

She backed away. "What did my leaving matter?

We said goodbye already. You're leaving next week. I had no reason to stay in Saplingville."

He took two steps, and pulled her into his arms. "I was sure I knew what I wanted, I planned my life carefully. It wasn't my design to fall in love with you, but I did. Please say you'll marry me."

Dottie wiggled out of his embrace and walked to the window. She paused, and turned to face him. "No, Victor. I won't be the reason you give up your dream. You'll resent me for the rest of your life."

He walked to her and searched her eyes for the love he'd seen only a few weeks ago. "No, the only thing I'll resent is if I let you go. Success and dreams are nothing without you. It's time for us to make some dreams together. Please give me a chance." He took a deep breath and swallowed. "I love you, Dottie."

"Victor, I've longed to hear you say those words, but how can I believe you?" Tears streamed down her face.

He fished in his pockets for a handkerchief and wiped her cheeks. "Believe me, Dottie, my life will be empty without you. What is the use of me following my dream if I don't have you?"

"Are you sure?"

He put his hand under her chin. "I'm sure I love you, and I'm sure I want to spend my life with you." Victor knelt on one knee. "Dottie Lester, will you marry me?"

She smiled and pulled him up to face her. "I love you, Victor Douglas."

He stared and swallowed. "I love you more." His heart raced. "But you didn't answer me."

She grinned. "Yes, I'll marry you."

He kissed her and scooped her into his arms. "You've made me the happiest man in the world."

Bess came in the room and cleared her throat. He put her down.

Dottie took his hand. "Aunt Bess, Victor asked me to marry him."

Bess rested her chin on her hands. "Congratulations. I wish Carolyn was here."

"She is. She's with me in everything I do," Dottie said as she wiped tears from both cheeks.

Bess glanced out the window. "How did you get here Victor? I don't see a car."

"I flew my airplane, and landed at Miller Field. I hitched a ride from there. Can you take us to the airport so I can get Dottie home?"

Bess stared at her. "Dottie, have you flown before?"

"Yes, Victor's taken me several times. I love to fly."

"Oh, goodness, please be careful."

He pulled her close. "I'm always careful, especially when my girl's with me. I'll take you for a ride sometime."

"I'll have to give it a lot of thought. I will take you both to the airport, if that's how y'all want to get home."

Dottie's smile lit up the room. "Yes, that's how I want to go home."

The flight to Saplingville from Macon didn't take long. Victor started his landing approach and noticed people standing on each side of the runway anticipating their arrival. He turned off the engine, got out of the plane and helped his fiancé out of her seat. Everyone gathered.

Walter shook his hand. "No one wanted to leave, they all wanted to stay and see if you brought Dottie with you."

He grabbed his girl and pulled her close. "I have an announcement to make. I asked Miss Dottie Lester to marry me." He paused staring at his family and friends. "She said yes."

Clapping with whoops and hollers erupted. Avery embraced them both.

Frankie yelled, "Does this mean you aren't leaving?"

"I'm not leaving, and if the offer from Uncle Walter is still good, and Frankie if you'll work for me, this very place we are standing will become Andrews Field."

Walter shook his head. "No sir, the name should be Douglas Field."

Victor turned and placed his hands on Walter's shoulders. "Uncle Walter, the airport's your idea. This land has been in the Andrews family for generations. The new airport will be called Andrews Field."

A word about the author…

Before fulfilling her dream of being a published romance writer, Jane Lewis worked as a freelance musician and teacher, and an analyst and manager for a large railroad company. She is a native of Atlanta and lover of all things southern. She graduated from Kennesaw State University, Kennesaw, Georgia, with a Bachelor of Arts degree in Music.

When she isn't writing her next romance, she enjoys cooking, tending her rose garden, playing music, yoga, and bowling with her real-life hero, her husband. She and her husband live in a suburb outside of Atlanta.

She is a PRO member of Romance Writers of America and Georgia Romance Writers. She was a 2016 finalist in the Hearts Through History, Post-Victorian/World War II category for her first romance novel, *Love At Five Thousand Feet*.

~*~

www.janelewisauthor.com
https://www.facebook.com/janelewisauthor/
https://twitter.com/janelewisauthor
https://www.pinterest.com/janelewis9917/

Thank you for purchasing
this publication of The Wild Rose Press, Inc.

If you enjoyed the story, we would appreciate your
letting others know by leaving a review.

For other wonderful stories,
please visit our on-line bookstore at
www.thewildrosepress.com.

For questions or more information
contact us at
info@thewildrosepress.com.

The Wild Rose Press, Inc.
www.thewildrosepress.com

Stay current with The Wild Rose Press, Inc.

Like us on Facebook

https://www.facebook.com/TheWildRosePress

And Follow us on Twitter
https://twitter.com/WildRosePress